To Brad

Norwesen
2012

THE SUMMONING

Muffy Morrigan

three
ravens

First Edition 2011

three
ravens

www.threeravensbooks.com
www.muffymorrigan.com

Cover design by Gina Gibson

Library of Congress Cataloging-In-Publication Data
is available upon request

ISBN 13: 978-0-9844356-5-4
ISBN 10: 0-9844356-5-4

One

Galen

The sun was shining through the windows, catching the massive quartz crystal that stood in one corner and casting a rainbow across the room in a sparkling arc of light. The warmth intensified the scents of the many herbs, oils and candles in the shop, and it all blended together creating an atmosphere that was both welcoming and comforting. There were other, hidden, things that offered a sense of protection that was very real, an invisible wall that kept unwanted things outside.

Galen Emrys watched the coffee stand across the street. His brother, Rob, was over getting their second round of coffees for the day. They had a coffeemaker of their own, but they both preferred the coffee from the stand, and Rob had an ulterior motive. He and the owner of Hot Babes Coffee were tentatively starting a relationship. Becci was all for it, and Galen agreed with her, but after the disturbing events of the past winter, Rob had withdrawn into himself.

The lingering aftermath of the attack by the

feorhbealu were at the root of it, Galen knew. His brother was normally reserved, but not withdrawn. As *Custodes Noctis,* Keepers of the Night, they shared a psychic bond that allowed them to sense the other, communicate silently and survive wounds that would otherwise kill them. Individually, they had Gifts as well, Galen as the elder brother was Gifted with healing, Rob with the Sight, allowing him to see things beyond the everyday world—the supernatural world, the auras of every living thing, Galen even suspected his brother had a Gift for seeing the past and future, although they had never spoken of it.

Or so it should have been.

During the final battle with the *feorhbealu*, their leader had targeted Rob and stripped him of his Gifts in an attempt to stop the *Custodes Noctis* and the riders of the Hunt from finishing the fight. It hadn't worked—at least not as they planned. The Hunt was victorious, and the *feorhbealu* were driven back through the Veil, the invisible wall between worlds.

Rob had been gravely injured, and while Galen had dealt with most of the physical injuries, he could not heal the wounds done to Rob's Gift. The best he had managed was to keep a small hum of their bond alive, enough to keep them functioning. They had both had the chance to exist without the bond—something that usually resulted in death for *Custodes Noctis*—during the years Galen had been "dead" after their first encounter with the Old One of the Legacy. That separation was enabling them to survive now.

They were still efficient fighters. Maybe even more so, without the full Gift to rely on, they were more aware and their skills were honed now to a sharpness Galen had never dreamed they would achieve. Most *Custodes Noctis* never lived to acquire that level of skill, they were usually killed in battle long before. Even now in the modern age when the things they fought were fewer and far between, Keepers died young.

They'd had a close call shortly after their ride with the Hunt and the battle with the *feorhbealu* when Galen has nearly been killed by a drunk driver. He'd been heading home after a gig with his band, The Urban Werewolves, when his Jeep had been side-swiped by a driver that ran a red light. Thankfully, his brother and Becci were in the car behind him; they'd witnessed the accident but escaped injury. In the hours immediately after, however, Galen had been sedated and on life support. Rob had barely held on, Galen still wondered exactly how his brother had managed. They hadn't talked about it. Every time he brought up the accident, Rob flinched, closed down and walked away. His brother was quiet and studious, but since the attack and the accident his brother was completely closed, unwilling to discuss either incident..

Galen picked up the polishing cloth and pulled off his bracelet—one of the symbols of his rank as *Custodes Noctis*. The seemingly simple band of copper, bronze and silver was the oldest of all the designs worn by the various families of Keepers. Each member of the *Custodes Noctis* received their bracelet on their thirteenth birthday when they returned from fosterage to study with their father and uncle as Tradition dictated. Keepers were separated by five years, allowing the elder brother to begin his training his skills as a healer before he went to retrieve his younger brother nine days before his thirteenth birthday. More than just metal, the bracelets were also woven with magic and bound to the wearer. When Rob's had been made, Galen had taken extra pains with it, carefully weaving in protection.

He looked up, Rob was heading back across the street. Galen put away the cloth—a sure sign he was worrying—and turned to the shelf with herbs, planning on straightening them, only to discover Rob had been there before him. They were arranged in alphabetical order, by Latin name, and he noticed his brother had added the names in several different languages as well. Galen snorted, he really doubted he would have anyone coming in looking for valerian and calling it by its Old Norse name.

"That better not be more than a quad," he said as Rob entered the shop.

"Becci won't sell me anything more than quads. Four shots of espresso at a time, it's all I get." Rob grinned.

"What does that mean?"

"You never said I couldn't have one when I was over there."

"So you've already had four?"

"Uh, well..."

"So that one makes how many?" Galen sighed. "Your heart is going to explode."

"Actually this one makes sixteen. It's better than drinking a couple of pots of coffee." Rob set the coffees down on the counter. "And I can talk to Becci, it's goth day."

"Oh." Galen smiled. When Becci Anderson had purchased the coffee stand it hadn't done well, until she had hit on the idea of Hot Babes Coffee. After enlisting the help of several like-minded women, they had turned the small stand into one of the most popular coffee stops in Tacoma, which was saying a lot in the coffee-flooded Northwest. While competitors complained it was because of the way they dressed, what made them popular was good coffee and good, fast service. Becci had made enough to open another stand, and Galen was proud of her.

"Did that order come in yet?" Rob asked.

"Did you see a truck?" Galen narrowed his eyes. "What's in it?" he asked suspiciously.

"Nothing."

"Nothing like?"

"Nothing like a 1534 folio of *Saxo Grammaticus*."

"Of course not."

"I ordered a new translation too," Rob added with a grin.

"So you could mock them?"

"Me? Mock?"

"Yes." Galen couldn't help grinning back. His brother's ability with languages still surprised him. By Galen's count his brother could read at least eighteen languages, ancient and modern, with the same ease most people read the newspaper. He also spoke most of them idiomatically; in fact, when they had first met the Riders of the Hunt, Rob had been able to communicate with them without any magical aid. After that first meeting, Galen had endured his brother's long-winded complaints about one of his history professors and his pronunciation. "Not only will you mock, you will probably write a paper about it."

"I only did that once," Rob said defensively. "And that idiot Robinson had the translation completely wrong. There is a vast difference between a lake and the sea, it changes the whole... Stop grinning at me. He was wrong."

"I'm sure he was." Galen picked up his coffee.

There were dark circles under his brother's eyes. He knew Rob didn't sleep much, in fact some nights not at all, but there was something else going on. The few hours his brother did manage were being disturbed by something, and without the bond, Galen had no idea what it was. Rob had cried out loud enough to wake him the night before, through closed doors and down the hall. By the time Galen reached his brother's room, Rob was awake, and out of bed. Rob hadn't gone back to sleep, either. The careful arrangement of candles in the storeroom attested to that fact.

Before he could figure out a way to broach the subject, a harsh croak from the rear entry interrupted him. Galen got up and headed into the back to open the door. Two ravens looked up at him innocently, keys dangling from one beak and part of a windshield wiper from the other. They were the King's Ravens, pledged to serve the King of the Hunt and his Champion. Since their induction into the Hunt, Rob was now King, Galen stood as Champion. The ravens had decided after centuries in the Between World, they wanted to follow Rob and Galen home and "serve" them there. Although Galen suspected they were just bored and looking for a new place to cause mischief. Ravens, by nature, were troublemakers.

Thousand-plus-year-old, supernatural ravens were at least a thousand times worse. Once they were home, the ravens had told Galen and Rob their names; their long, long names—apparently they added a title and a name for each king they served. After attempting to pronounce the multisyllabic tongue twisters several times, Rob had asked if they could call them Ealdor—meaning elder, and

Federa—meaning uncle. The ravens had agreed, even allowing the further shortening to Dor and Dera. Their current favorite pastime was annoying Galen's friend and bandmate, Flash, by dismantling his car and stealing his keys on a regular basis.

"Oh, Flash is going to be pissed," Rob said from behind him.

"He enjoys the game," Dera's deep bass spoke in Galen's head. He was still getting used to the idea of the birds speaking to him.

"I really doubt that," Galen chided. Dera had chosen to serve him as King's Champion whereas Dor preferred, and served Rob, who was King.

Dor chuckled and fluttered up onto one of the stools, dropping the keys. Dera followed suit and they both looked up expectantly. "I left dinner on the counter," Rob told them. "Galen tried to put it in the fridge." He paused while Dor clacked his beak with derision. "He said he might want it for breakfast." Dera shook his head sadly and made a small croaking sound, then the two of them flew up the stairwell towards the apartment over the shop.

"I was planning on eating it," Galen said.

"The ravens like Thai food."

"They like everything, Brat." Galen headed back into the shop.

"True, it's all good after the Between World. Dor told me everything tasted the same." Rob looked up as a customer came in and smiled. "Can I help you?" he asked, putting on his "shop face."

The flow of customers was steady through the day. The shop had a wide cross-section of customers and both Galen and Rob were kept busy. In addition to people coming in to purchase tangible items, Galen had a small side business as a healer. His great-great grandfather had been the first Emrys healer in Tacoma, when the town was in its infancy, and the tradition continued. The shop was in the same place, although over the years the offerings had been expanded to include magical and medicinal herbs, jewelry and other, more esoteric, items. After Rob had come home, they had added a small research "library" with books that were not for sale, but that customers could use under his watchful eye.

Becci stopped in at three with coffee for them, and by the time they were ready to close the door, Galen was exhausted. Three clients had been in that day, and all three had needed more than just a simple healing. Each one took a little more and by closing, all he could do was sit behind the counter and watch Rob balance the till and lock up for the night.

"You want to go up to Gateway for dinner?" Rob asked, frowning at him.

"Um..." Galen was having a hard time focusing.

"Come on." Rob tugged him off the stool. "A walk will help, it always does." The Indian restaurant was only a few blocks from the shop. "Let's go."

Galen followed his brother out into the warm evening. Since the accident, healing caused a odd and uncomfortable ache in the scar the Old One of the Legacy had left when it had ripped itself out of his chest. He wasn't sure why, there was really no relation to the two, but it was there, throbbing along his sternum. After several deep breaths he felt a little better and by the time they walked into the restaurant he was feeling almost normal.

The hostess recognized them and waved them towards their usual table towards the back of the room.

Galen preferred it because, unless it was crowded, they were far enough away from the other diners so that he didn't get a wash of their emotions while he tried to relax and eat. When he was tired it was harder to block that part of the Gift, while still keeping the remnants of the bond as open as possible.

"Your damn birds ate my car," someone said, sliding into the seat across the table from him.

"I hardly think taking part of the windshield wiper counts as eating the car, Flash," Rob replied, glancing at the menu.

"They're a menace," Flash growled.

"You tell them." Rob looked up when the waitress came by and ordered dinner.

"No fucking way. It's creepy knowing the damn birds *can* talk to me at all. It still traumatizes me on a daily basis. I'm not starting the damn conversation. Hey, are you okay?" Flash's tone changed as he glanced over at Galen.

"Yeah, I just had three clients today," Galen assured him.

"Three clients is stupid. You know that, ever since..." Flash trailed off. He'd been riding with Rob and Becci the night of the accident.

"One was an emergency."

"I don't care, and as Chief Vassal Guy, I get to say." Flash had followed them into battle with the Hunt, and as a reward for his "bravery and loyal service in battle" as the Sagas said, Galen and Rob had named him Chief Vassal, a title not bestowed on anyone by a member of the *Custodes Noctis* for centuries. Flash proudly wore his vassal's bracelet, similar to the bracelets Galen and Rob wore, indicating his fealty to their line.

"It's okay," Galen assured him.

"I doubt it." Flash glared at him for another moment, then turned his gaze on Rob. "About those damn birds..."

"I can't tell them anything, they do what they want," Rob said calmly.

"You're the king!"

"And you think that means they'll listen to me?" Rob laughed. "When there's something interesting going on?"

"Why is the *interesting* my car?"

"Probably because you play their game."

"I so do not," Flash grumbled. "Okay, maybe a little, but the windshield wiper is the last straw! They took it apart, I have to get a whole new piece."

"We'll pay for it," Rob offered.

Galen listened to the interplay, he wasn't sure when he realized it, but something was off in his brother. There was a gray tinge to his skin that was worrying, and the dark circles he'd noticed earlier in the day were more prominent. He tried to force the bond open further, hoping he could get a glimmer of what was happening. As he reached out he encountered a wall, as solid as stone, and for one blinding instant he was sure the wall actually shoved back.

"Galen?" Flash asked, concern in his voice.

"Yeah?" He blinked, the restaurant came back into focus. "Sorry."

"What happened?"

Galen was saved from answering when the waitress brought the food. Rob and Flash started up their argument about the ravens again, and Galen tried to get a handle on what he'd caught in that brief contact through the bond. Whatever it was, it had been completely alien to his brother, and he had the strangest sense that it had been intelligent, something lurking deep within Rob that Galen had never seen before. It was something new or he would have sensed it. Prior to their battle with the Hunt, the bond had been strong enough for them to communicate easily, so nothing could have hidden itself. Even though his brother had the unnerving ability to make something "true" or read as true through the bond if he believed what he was doing was right. Galen knew nothing like this could have been lurking. This did not feel right in any way. In fact, Galen had the fleeting impression that Rob might not even be consciously aware of it.

"You think if I take the damn birds the rest of my food they'll leave my car alone?" Flash's voice broke into his musings.

"I think if you stopped calling them names it would help," Rob replied.

"Bribes always help. Right, Galen?" When Galen didn't answer immediately Flash glanced over at him. "You okay?"

"What?"

"Galen?" Rob grabbed his wrist. "What's going on?"

"Are you okay?" Galen countered, meeting his brother's slate-blue eyes.

"What do you mean?"

"Yeah?" Flash said, looking between the two of them.

"Rob?"

His brother sighed, letting out a breath like he'd been holding it for a long, long time. "I don't know, Galen. I think... I think I might be losing my mind."

Two

Rob

There was nothing. The darkness was complete and silent, it was as if he was encased in a tomb of impenetrable material that nothing could breach, not even air. After attempting to draw several unsuccessful, panicked breaths, Rob jerked awake, gasping for air. He covered his face with shaking hands, the dream was more frequently terrorizing his few hours of sleep. Running a hand through his hair, he took a slow, deep breath, trying to center himself the way Galen had shown him when they were young. It was hard, though, the sensation of being buried alive still very much with him, and controlling that primal terror was almost impossible at the moment.

Knowing there was no chance he would get back to sleep, Rob got out of bed and wandered through the silent apartment. He paused by Galen's door long enough to make sure he hadn't disrupted his brother's sleep again. The last couple of nights his scream brought Galen running, and trying to talk his way around that was getting more difficult. If Rob knew what was going on, he'd tell his brother, in fact once or twice he'd almost blurted it out anyway, but as it was, there didn't seem to be any point. Sometimes, when he first woke, it felt solid enough to get a handle on, strong enough to heed what felt like a summons, but then it would disappear like dreams did—or so he heard. Mostly he remembered his dreams. So, he guessed it was some leftover memory surfacing from those days when he'd been buried alive as one of the rituals for the Old One of the Legacy. There *was* something in his current dream that seemed almost familiar, almost like that, Rob concentrated, trying to bring the dream into clearer focus, but it was already slipping away.

He padded downstairs. He'd use the coffeemaker in the shop so he wouldn't wake Galen. When he'd first moved home, his brother had only one pot, upstairs in the kitchen. After discovering nothing woke Galen faster than the smell of freshly brewing coffee, Rob had purchased another coffeemaker for downstairs to keep him company on his nocturnal watches. He got the coffee brewing, and walked through the shop, turning on the open sign and unlocking the door. Over the last couple of years, he'd developed a night-only clientele and they were used to him being available several evenings a week.

Rob loved the shop at night. It felt entirely different, the energies that flowed through the building—through the world—were different when the sun was down. Before his Gift had been taken he'd been able to see the difference as well, the soft glows that ebbed and flowed around everything changing color, and what he thought of as temperature, at night. The world really was a different and changed place when the sun set, and he always felt like it was a place he belonged.

That might have been because of the Sight. Even when he was a small child, the night was never pitch black, everything had some small energy glowing around it, and until he'd learned to control his Gift, it had continued to grow until he was assaulted every moment. He'd started his nightly vigils then, when he was in his middle teens. Galen was dead, or so he believed, and he was the only Keeper to survive the severing of the bond. Of course, his father and uncle assured him that it was because he and Galen had never performed the Ritual of the Swords, the formal bonding as warriors, as *Custodes Noctis*. Rob knew better. He had known the instant Galen's heart had stopped—he should, he'd been the one who'd stopped it, and he knew that for a moment he'd died too, dropping into a gentle shimmering lake. When he woke to discover the lake—and the bond with his brother—gone, he'd been mired in grief for a long time. Without the formal training, his already powerful Gift had gotten out of control and he'd gone searching for answers.

Thinking of that, he glanced at the clock and pulled out his phone. Billy Hernandez, the shaman who'd helped him on his first faltering steps towards controlling his Gift, would still be up at this hour. The older man only slept between moon-set and sunrise, and according to the calendar Galen had hanging behind the cash register, the moon didn't set until three.

"Rob?" Billy answered before there was a ring on Rob's end of the phone. "What is it?" No preamble, no chit-chat, the shaman knew if there was a late-night call there was a reason.

"I think I've been dreaming."

"Think?"

"I'm not sure, it's more physical sensation."

"Hmm," Billy said. Rob could picture him, leaning forward, listening with his whole body. "What do you mean exactly?"

"I think I've been dreaming about being buried alive."

"You keep saying you think, are you unsure of the content?" Billy's voice was thoughtful.

"No, I know I'm buried, I am just not sure..." Rob trailed off, trying to catch any of the slivers of the dream again, but they were gone.

"If it's a dream at all?" the shaman offered. "Is it a sending?"

"That's what I'm not sure of, I can't tell. It's gone before I can get a hold of it. Since I lost the Gift..."

"Rob!" Billy cut him off sharply. "You have to remember that you don't need that Gift to walk in the other Worlds. You have become too focused on this loss. I am not *Custodes Noctis* and I know some of your other guides weren't as well. So, tell me what you can."

"It's dark, pitch black, no light, nothing." He took a slow breath, reaching in to find what he could. "There's no sound, and I can't breathe."

"Is there more?"

"Yes, but I can't remember."

"You can't remember?" Billy repeated. "You've tried?"

"I have, but even if I try as soon as I start to wake up it's gone. It's almost like..." Rob paused, thinking about it.

"Something's blocking you?"

"That's just it, I don't know. I don't even know if it's just a dream or something else."

"You called me." Billy laughed. "You obviously

think it's more than just a dream."

"I do, I'm not sure what it is, though. It's... It... Well, it feels almost like the Old One."

"How so?" Billy's voice was concerned.

"I can't be sure, there is a familiar feeling about it. Could it just be a memory?"

"Does it feel like a memory?"

"No, it doesn't, not really. There are echoes of the Old One, but this feels different. I think I've just convinced myself it must be a memory because of what happened."

"But, Rob," Billy said gently, "when you were buried as part of the ritual, it wasn't completely dark, you could hear and you could breathe—the scent of the incense is a key part of that memory."

"So what is it? Fear of the loss of my Gift?"

"If that was it you would have been having the dreams for a lot longer."

"Okay, Billy, what?"

"I don't know. Let me do a little work here. The next time you sleep, try to guide it if you can."

"I wish you were here," Rob said softly.

"If you need me, I will be," the shaman answered. "I will see if I can find more of what might be disturbing you. Have you spoken with Galen?"

"No."

"Why not?"

Rob thought about that for a minute, all the reasons he'd used to convince himself about why he hadn't mentioned the disturbing dreams to his brother. "I'm not ready."

"Hmm, I'm not sure I like that answer," Billy said thoughtfully. "I'll do some work on this and talk to you tomorrow. If you sleep before then, call me."

"I will."

"Promise me, I need the words, Rob, I need this bound."

"What's going on?"

"Just do it."

"I will call you if I sleep, I give my word, honor bound," Rob said solemnly, breaking the connection. Something tugged at the edge of his awareness as he spoke the words. He focused on it, trying to chase it down, but whatever it had been moved quickly out of his awareness.

"Hey? You around?" Borja, one of Rob's regular customers called from the front of the shop.

"Yeah, you want coffee?"

"Only reason I come by, you know that."

Rob laughed and poured two cups of coffee and carried them out, handing one to the dark-haired man. "I got a new blend in, Becci ordered it special."

"I liked that last one, but you're always looking for the perfect cup. You're like one of those wine guys."

"I am not, well, maybe a little." He sat down on the stool behind the counter. "When you drink as much as I do, you get picky."

"I bet."

"What brings you by tonight?" Rob asked.

"I need aconite, belladonna and a silver charm." Borja sipped the coffee while Rob pulled the herbs off the shelf. "You've added to the labels."

"I have, I found a couple references in a Saga to magical plants used in Northern Europe and followed them back, I'm pretty sure these are the right terms in a proto-Uralic dialect."

"I doubt someone is going to wander in to correct you."

"You might be surprised."

"No, not really." Borja glanced around the shop. "The world is changing."

"It always is."

"No, Rob, there is *something* happening, I've been more aware of it since last winter, when you and Galen were gone. I know you were fighting something Old, something that is Not Seen." The man put emphasis on the words, he understood the world—worlds. While most people saw Borja as a dark-haired, polite Native American, in reality he was only half that. The other half was a shifter, able to see into the Between World and at certain times of the year walk there.

"Do you know what it is?" Rob asked, looking up from the collection of silver charms.

"I'm not sure, something Old is moving, and I..." He met Rob's eyes. "I can't tell you everything, but I have seen something coming. I saw a desecration, I saw twisted metal and I saw Darkness there. I don't know what it means. It was not a place I recognized."

"But?"

"You are involved, I sensed you there."

"Me?" Rob set the charms on the counter. "Which one?"

Borja closed his eyes and let his hand run over the pieces. "This one."

"I just got it in yesterday."

"Which is why I am here today," Borja said, smiling. "That and the coffee." He leaned against the counter. "The vision, it's mixed up. You should know that. The time line is skewed in a way I've never experienced before." Shaking his head, he sighed. "I wish I could tell you more, but the world is changing, and not the way most expect."

"Yeah, I think so too. There was a mention in one of the Sagas. I'm trying to track it down, about one of the Old Ones, it was just a line or two. I need more information before I can make any conclusions."

"Those who were here Before." Borja nodded. "They are why you are here."

"The Keepers."

"No, you and your brother." The man grinned and finished his coffee. "Never doubt." He paid for his items and left.

Rob watched him go then poured himself another cup and wandered over to the books. They needed re-arranging. He pulled all the books off the shelves, dusted the wood and considered them for a minute. After deciding how he would arrange them, he began re-shelving them, letting his mind drift. He'd discovered a long time ago that if his hands were occupied he could focus his mind and chase things that were less tangible with greater ease. One of his professors had explained it during a lecture, a long, boring lecture, but the fact was Rob found it easier to meditate if his hands had something to do. He'd never been one for just sitting and thinking. Maybe it was because of those hours he'd been trapped as a child. Or maybe... He shoved that memory away, not ready to face it tonight.

Once he had the books in the order he wanted, he turned to the storeroom. They'd received several large orders that hadn't been completely gone through. Galen had checked the packing slips, but left the rest for Rob to take care of during his nocturnal shopkeeping. Rob opened the first box and started going through it, carefully arranging items in piles that he would move either into the shop or onto the storeroom shelves. Halfway through the second box, he found several books he'd ordered for his research collection. He made the mistake of opening one of them, and the rest of the sorting was forgotten as he began reading.

"How long have you been sitting there?" Galen asked, coming down the stairs.

"What?" Rob looked up, the soft light of a rainy morning was coming through the back window. "Uh..." Glancing at the pile of books beside him, he frowned. "Two books?"

"You've been sitting there for two books?" His brother sighed. "English? Or something else?"

"One English, one Latin, so not too long, I don't think." Rob stood and stretched. His left foot was asleep, he wiggled it to get the blood flowing again. "I'll go get coffee." He realized the pot he'd made the night before wasn't empty. Or was that the second pot? He'd been so absorbed in reading, he'd completely lost track of the time.

"I was expecting it to be waiting," Galen said, giving him an odd look.

Rob smiled and walked through the shop. It was drizzling, a typical Northwest drizzle, although it was warm. He wasn't sure if that made it better or worse. It made Galen happy because the plants loved it and Rob had endured his brother's enthusiastic explanations about how plants preferred rain to hand watering. He personally suspected it had more to do with his brother's Gifts than the rain, but he just let Galen talk. The morning air was heavy with the scent of coffee, flowers and rain. Rob couldn't help smiling as he headed across the street.

"Morning, Rob, you're late," Becci said, sliding the window open. "I've had one ready for ten minutes."

"Thanks." He pulled her down for a quick kiss before taking the cup, leaning against the stand and waiting for her to make more. "I was reading."

"I saw the light on in the back. I almost knocked, but I was running a little late and the boss is a bitch."

"You're the boss," Rob said, grinning at her.

"I know, right?" She laughed and started Galen's mocha. "How was business last night?"

"Borja dropped by, but that's all. I spent most of the night unpacking orders."

"Until you found some books?"

"Well, yeah, until then. They were for the research section, and I've been waiting for them, but I wanted to make sure they were okay before I put them out."

"You mean you wanted to play with your toys before anyone else?" Becci giggled, the smile lighting her eyes in the way that made Rob's heart flutter.

"Something like that. Thanks, Becci, I'll be back in a bit." He took the coffees she handed him and headed across the street.

Galen was at the bookshelves, frowning at them. He took the cup. "So, what's the new system this time?"

"I think it's pretty obvious."

"Uh huh."

"Top three shelves, magic. Herbs, charms, other, then subdivided by region, so Europe, Asia... Next shelves are herbals that can fall into magic and medicine, again subdivided by region, all alphabetized by author. It's the same for all the other subjects as well." He glanced at Galen. "I color coded them too."

"Oh, is that why my bookshelves look like they have the measles?"

"I was thinking polka dots, it was Becci's idea. She thought it would make it easier for some of our more casual clients to come and find a book. All the, ahem, less serious books are in the pink dot section."

"Becci's idea?"

"No, she wanted little daisies. I thought the pink was less noticeable."

From the sound of mock disgust, he was pretty sure Galen would have preferred the daisies. "At least I know it will all change in a week or two."

"You never know."

"Did you sleep last night?" Galen asked, casually walking over to the counter and sitting down. His brother rarely commented on his sleeping habits.

"I did, for a little while. Something woke me and I couldn't get back to sleep."

"Are we going to talk about the something?"

"Yes." Rob took a drink of coffee.

"Now?"

"I'm not sure it's a something that's anything yet."

"Dor told Dera that you couldn't breathe."

"How do they know? They weren't even there!" Rob stopped, realizing he'd just said more than he should have.

"And the late night call was to...?"

"Billy."

"Why?" Galen was completely focused on him. Rob had always suspected his brother had some tiny hint of the Sight, maybe not even enough to consciously realize it, but that searching look was more intense than usual.

"I'm not sure, Galen. I don't know if it's a dream or a

memory or what. Billy has helped in that past, before I came home, you know that." He took a breath to defend himself, but his brother just nodded for him to continue. "And Borja came in last night and said something was coming, something Old and it would involve me—us— and some now and some later. He said the time line was 'skewed'."

"Skewed? That's odd from a shifter. Usually they see visions as a linear projection."

"I know, he said there was twisted metal, desecration and Darkness, capital D type."

"And we're involved? Keepers or us?"

"He said us, although I have a feeling it's bigger than that," Rob said, sifting through the conversation again.

"What is? The now or the later?"

"I have only had eight shots of espresso, ask me after ten more."

"And that's supposed to make me feel better?"

"No." Rob sigh. "It doesn't make me feel better either. There's something wrong, Galen. I just don't know if it's me or the world or both."

THREE

Galen

The garden was quiet, the warm scent of the richness of growing things surrounded Galen as he knelt among his plants, gently pulling some to transplant to the other side, or snipping a leaf to encourage growth. He never weeded the garden in the sense most people would, he just coaxed the plants up and moved them to a different area. One person's weed was someone else's medicinal or magical plant. He still laughed at the memory of Flash's discovery of the carefully tended patch of dandelions. Even after Galen had carefully explained that they were important, and not just "filthy pain-in-the-ass weeds", Flash remained unconvinced. In fact, after sitting with Galen while he tended the garden once or twice, his friend had become so frustrated he'd disappeared to the coffee stand for nearly an hour.

Galen really couldn't blame him. Flash wasn't really made for sitting and talking to plants, and his idea of taking care of a yard involved a power lawnmower that was capable of mowing down everything including small trees and probably small cars if they got in the way. Still, Flash had hovered over Galen while he was getting the garden ready in early Spring.

Everyone had hovered, reaction to the accident, no doubt. It had taken Galen months to get his brother and friends to allow him time alone. He was fine, he'd healed. Rob should know better, but, then again, Galen was still haunted by injuries Rob had suffered and he knew, objectively at least, that his brother was fine. The subjective mind wasn't so sure.

He'd retreated to the garden to think, the space offered more than something to do. The area was Bolted, nothing supernatural could enter or even gaze in without his permission. The ravens could come and go as they pleased, and he was usually surprised by some small gift they'd found and left among the plants. Today he'd discovered a piece of what looked like brightly colored beads tucked in the gray lamb's ears. They were adding their own magic to the garden, at least he hoped that's what it was. He did know there was a peace here that was nowhere else, a quiet in his heart and mind that let him think.

There was a lot to think about. Something was going on, he'd noticed his brother's odd sleeping habits were even more erratic than usual, and judging by the hyper-organizing of the shop, Rob was on edge. The fact his brother had called Billy Hernandez was a little worrying. Galen was trying not to let it bother him that Rob had called Billy rather than talk with him, but he knew Rob and the shaman had worked together when Galen was "dead" and it was a natural reaction. Even if it stung. He was trying to trust Rob to let him know what was going on, but there was a nagging sense of foreboding that

Galen knew was more than just misplaced worry.

He knew they had Gifts that were different than many other *Custodes Noctis;* actually according to Rob, they had the Gifts that the Keepers once had, but had been put aside for various reasons ranging from the fact they were viewed as "dangerous" to "just not needed" in the modern world. The Scientific Revolution had affected the *Custodes Noctis* , and even though they knew Darkness still walked the earth, many families had cast aside many of the Traditions, keeping only those that seemed to fit in a world ruled by science. For some reason, Galen and Rob still had those lost Gifts. Some of them were obvious, Rob had a small Gift of healing—or had before his encounter with the *feorhbealu,* and Galen had a tiny bit of the Sight. Nothing like his brother's Gift, but enough to help boost his healing and enough to see the dark shadow lurking behind his brother for the last few days.

Galen wished he had something to compare that shadow with, but when he looked directly at it, the thing disappeared. If he brushed a hand into it, there was nothing there, so whatever it was, it was not physically there. At least not in the world they were in. It could be just behind the Veil, hiding behind the curtain that divide the worlds, but Galen still should be able to touch it. Sighing, he leaned against the bench, carefully transplanting several small sweet cicely plants that had started under the comfrey. Maybe he was imaging the whole thing.

"There is something wrong," Dera's deep voice said as the raven landed on the bench, nudging Galen's cheek almost like a cat.

"What do you mean?" Galen replied, stroking the

bird's silky feathers.

"We do not fear darkness, we have flown in the Between World, but something wakes that frightens many things. The Riders fear what is coming."

"The Riders? You mean the Hunt? You've been out to the Hunt?"

"Gaius sent a message: 'Tell the King and his Champion that something rises, tell them it comes for them, tell them it was foretold in the Saga'."

Gaius Emrys was their ancestor, the last Emrys to join the Hunt voluntarily until Galen and Rob. He still rode in the Between World helping the Riders stay loyal to the *Custodes Noctis* and not stray into evil. "Did he mention which Saga?"

"No." Dera clacked his beak together in disgust. Galen couldn't help but agree. There were hundreds of Sagas, and many had been lost since Gaius had been alive and studied them. For all they knew, the Saga they needed wasn't even available anymore. *"Should we ask?"*

"Rob?" Galen asked, the raven nodded. "If it's an obscure Saga, he'll know it. There's something going on with him. The dreams he's having, I think they are tied up with this thing."

"We agree, it's why we watch." Dera cocked his head to the side like he was listening to something, then with a curt nod at Galen fluttered up into the sky.

Wondering what brought about the raven's abrupt exit, Galen stood, dusted the dirt from his hands and headed back towards the shop. He stopped at the sink and washed his hands, then headed into the front. Rob had several books on the counter in front of him. "Coffee?" Galen asked.

"Is the sky up?" Rob answered with a smile.

"I'll be right back." Galen walked over to the coffee stand, Becci and Sarah were both in the small booth, getting ready for shift change. They turned to Galen with a smile, Becci starting the coffee without even asking what he wanted.

"Is Flash coming by later?" Sarah tried to sound casual.

"I'm not sure, he tends to show up in time for food, but band practice is tomorrow," Galen said. Flash and Sarah had an almost-relationship. It was beginning to drive him a little crazy. Neither one of them would make more than a hesitant first move—it was getting to the point where he and Rob were planning a set-up of some kind and just locking the two in a room with dinner and a bottle of wine until they worked it out.

"Oh." Sarah pouted a little. "He was supposed to call."

"I'll remind him," Galen assured her, grabbing the coffees and heading back before he could get drawn into Flash's attempts at a love life.

"You look a little perturbed," Rob said, opening the door as Galen reached the shop.

"Flash was supposed to call Sarah. You're just lucky the coffees were finished."

"I would have forgiven you in that case." He took the cup Galen handed him. "I've been reading."

"Still?"

"No, these came in the shipment today, several of them I have been waiting impatiently for." Rob pulled him towards the counter. "Especially this one."

The book was old, Galen might even class it in the "ancient" class. The pages were obviously not paper, but vellum, the ink faded and the letters, though carefully uniform, were obviously penned by hand. It had the distinct scent of a vellum book, not the musty old paper, but something else, more organic. He brushed his hand over it, getting a sense of power that resonated off the book. It had been owned by someone in the past that had immense control of the supernatural world. "Do I want to know what this cost?"

"No," Rob said with a grin. "You really don't."

"What is it?"

"It's the *Fyrngidd Ealdféond*."

"Uh huh." Galen met his brother's slate-blue eyes. "A Saga?"

"Yes and no, it's a Saga, but it's also a prophecy of sorts."

"Of sorts? What does that mean?"

"It's a Saga of the Beginning Times, the time when the Old Ones walked the earth. Some of it speaks of the time before our grandfather's grandmother's grandfather's time."

"Meaning a long, long time," Galen offered.

"Pretty much. It's a mixture of creation myth with actual history. Some prophecy of things to come—some things which have already happened by the way—and some things yet to happen. There are thirteen books in total, this is one of the only ones that hasn't been lost, and this is, as far as I know, the oldest version extant." Rob's eyes were sparkling with excitement. "I know there *is* a lot of information missing, but this is fascinating. It tells of the founding of one of the other family lines of Keepers and how they joined with the Emrys family to fight in a battle 'at the place of the standing stones', I'm still trying to figure which place that is. Anyway, what's really interesting is the first part, from the myth-history part."

"You have had too much coffee." Galen couldn't help grinning. His brother was in his element and it had nothing to do with caffeine. "Well?"

Rob carefully turned the pages back to the beginning of the book, a large, ornately designed capital covered half the front page. "It talks about a war, the Old Ones were involved in the fight. The *feorhbealu* and something else, something I am still trying to track down, I think it must be in one of the other books. It's tied to the *Custodes Noctis* somehow and the bracelets were..."

"Rob!" Galen stopped him before he got off track.

"Oh, right, sorry. There was a war, and the Old Ones were involved, actually everything was. Looking at the various times, I think it might match up with the..."

"Rob?"

"Oh, yeah, war. There were two factions, well more than that, but two main ones, and some of the losing side suffered the..." Rob paused and ran his hand down the page. "They suffered 'the death that is not death, the death that remains forever, the death that is held motionless.'"

"What does that mean?"

"I'm not sure, it could be poetic, just to move the story along, or it could be something that actually happened. It all depends on that time line." Rob sighed. "I need to know when this particular war happened, it would help me figure out what was going on. I think... Hmm."

"What?"

"I'm not sure. I need more coffee."

"I just brought you more," Galen pointed out.

"You did, but it's never enough." Rob laughed. "I

wish I could figure out the whens of this thing. There's a translation of one of the only other parts, but I don't trust it."

"You don't trust anyone's translations."

"True, but it's one of those that has some fundamental errors from the outset," Rob said, leaning back and sipping his coffee.

"How can you be sure if you haven't seen the original?"

"Well, for one thing I know the translation is from a secondary source, a Latin translation done in the Sixteenth Century, that in and of itself raises a red flag."

"Not all Latin manuscripts are bad," Galen said, a little defensively. "I used several for my dissertation and they generally agreed with the older sources."

"They do, generally, but there is a difference in what we're dealing with here. You were using medical texts mostly. The Sagas and related works are different and a mistranslation of one word can lead to an entirely different meaning of the whole *Saga*! The single word can create a chain reaction that can lead to disaster." Rob paused, his eyes intense. "Most translators are thinking about it from a literary standpoint. They don't consider the reality of it. They want their translation to sound good to the modern reader, not necessarily be as accurate as possible. For example, in the *Saga of the Winter King* one of the modern translations lists the servants of the king as 'dark-plumed winged fae' and that's not quite right."

"Dera and Dor would agree with that."

"I realize that's something small, but that's just an example. Literary effect is great, but when it means the literal life-or-death difference for us or another pair of Keepers, I'm a little picky about the translation." He paced away from the counter and glanced out the window. "We both know how wrong it can be, and we both know what that can cost, so I..."

"Rob," Galen said softly.

"What?"

"Deep breath."

"Sorry." Rob wandered back over to the counter. "This is really bothering me, I know there are parts missing, and I have a funny feeling those parts are important. If I just knew what I needed I might be able to track it down through another history." Rob paused again, staring at the book. "Billy called."

"Oh?"

"When I talked to him last night he said he would do some checking on his end, to see what he could find out."

"About your dreams?" Galen asked.

"Or whatever they are, yeah. He did a Walk to see what he could find." Rob ran a hand through his hair. Galen noticed it was shaking. "Billy's been a lot of places, Galen..."

"I'm beginning to get the feeling I'm not going to like this."

"He said there was a wall, which is actually common on a Walk, but this wall wouldn't move. Billy tried to get past and whatever was there pushed him away. After that he tried to get a better look at where he was, but even that he couldn't pin down. Whatever it is, it's incredibly powerful."

"But what is it?"

"I don't know. In the dream it feels almost like the Old One."

"And we haven't mentioned that before because why?" Galen asked.

"Because I wasn't sure, because I do dream about what happened sometimes and it feels real, and this was close enough..."

Galen put a hand on his brother's arm, getting a sense of the emotions there. Even with the bond muted, he could still use the healing in the same way he would with a client. Rob wasn't lying, but he wasn't telling the whole truth either, however when Galen tried to throw open the bond a little further, something clamped it down, the briefest flash of a dark shadow, then it was gone. "What the hell....?" he muttered. Rob was right, for an instant it did have a feeling to it like the Old One that they'd faced, the same creature that had torn itself free of his body and left a deep scar on his chest. A scar that let him sense the darkness that moved under the earth, it was almost like a tether he could never escape. He'd thought after their ride with the Hunt it would stop, but it was still there and he could feel the deep thrum of the vile things lurking in the world.

"See?" Rob's voice was unsure.

"It's not the Old One we faced, and it's not a memory." Galen would have been able to move through the memory, and the thing they'd fought was dead, even though some of its servants still survived.

"No, it's not. I think it's one of their kind though, an Old One or something like it, left over from the Wars. That's why the date is so vital."

"What do you mean?"

"According to the Sagas, there were a series of Wars, before and after the founding of the *Custodes Noctis*. One of those led to the founding of the Hunt, right?"

"Yeah?"

"Well," Rob continued, "finding out which war this

creature fought in is important."

"Why?" Galen asked, the sense of foreboding growing, along with an ache in the scar on his chest.

"Because if it was one of the Ancient Ones, the *Ealdféond,* we're in big trouble."

"The Ancient Ones?" Galen knew his Sagas well enough to know what his brother was talking about. "I know they aren't myth, but I thought they were all gone, driven through the Veil or destroyed."

"I did too, but that's why this book is so important. Supposedly there was a dissenter, and he was punished with the death that isn't death."

"Which means?" Galen asked.

"I think it means he's here."

"Here?"

"Yeah, and somehow it's found me."

"Rob?"

"It's here." His brother turned back to the book. "And... 'thus it will come, after the time of fire and ice, it will come in the time of the heart, the heart that will beat in the everlasting death.'"

"That makes no sense."

"Let me finish." Rob looked up, his eyes bleak. "It goes on, 'the time of the one without what he was Gifted shall come and he shall be summoned.'"

"Rob..."

"It's me, Galen, face it. It's me."

FOUR

Rob

The scent of old vellum filled his senses, wisps of dust floated in the air and sparkled in the lamplight. Rob leaned back in his chair and stared at the ceiling. The coffee was starting to wear off, and he'd finally reached the point where he couldn't stomach the idea of another cup. He had considered several of the herbs on the shelves in the shop, thanks to Galen he knew which ones were stimulants. Realistically, he knew he needed sleep. It was getting to the point where he knew he'd pushed himself too far, stayed awake too long. Sighing, he stood, stretched and headed back towards his bedroom. After spending the afternoon and most of the evening head down in various books and manuscripts, Rob was past the point of being able to concentrate. He had too many words, too many Sagas running through his head to make sense of them any longer.

His room was quiet, this late at night there was very little traffic on Sixth Avenue and their bedrooms faced the parking area behind the shop rather than the street. Rob made sure the window was open enough for Dor to get in if he wanted to and laid down. He focused on his breathing trying to enter an "aware" dream state, as Billy had suggested, but he'd been up too long and before he managed to take his third breath he was asleep.

He was trapped in the dark, silent tomb, unable to breathe, every nerve in his body was screaming in terror, but he couldn't fight free of the place. It was death, but unlike the other death he'd known, instead of fighting it, he tried to sink into it. And suddenly he was through.

A dark landscape opened in front of him, rolling hills, and the scent of dust and dried grass was all around. The sweep of land had a dark path running through it, Rob stopped in shock when he realized that the path was bathed in an odd shine. He was seeing with his Gift, and the trail with its oily dark shine led along the hills towards a deep slash in the land. Bending down, he laid a hand on the ground. The path was pulsing, a slow, slow beat and as he stepped onto it, the entire world around him shivered. At the edge of his awareness, he thought he could hear a sound grating through the air. For an instant he thought he could hear his name being called. After waiting for a moment, he continued on.

"Rob!" He was physically yanked back and slammed against something hard. "Rob!" This time the word was accompanied by a hard shake.

"What?" Rob muttered, opening his eyes to glare at his brother, then feeling his breath catch in surprise. He was in the main room of the apartment at the top of the stairs. "How'd I get here?"

"You tell me," Galen said, stepping back. His dark green eyes were flashing with a combination of anger and fear. "You damn near went down the stairs. I caught you just in time."

"Huh?" Rob was completely disoriented, still caught partially on that path. When he looked down, he could see it shimmering at his feet, black oil running down the stairs.

"You almost went down the stairs," Galen repeated and pulled him, none too gently, across the living room and shoved him into a chair. "Want to tell me why?"

"Why?" Rob felt lost.

Galen frowned, his eyes narrowing. "What has you?" he asked, more to himself than Rob. He laid a hand over Rob's heart and one on his head in the Traditional healer's touch and the next moment Rob was flooded with the white light of the healing. It blasted the dream and confusion away. "Are you with me now?" Galen peered into his eyes.

"I..." Rob looked around. "I'm in the living room."

"We covered that."

"What happened?" Rob remembered the dream, the path and following it.

"I heard a noise and got up, lucky for you I did, because you were about to take a swan dive down the stairs."

"There weren't stairs in the dream," Rob said.

"You don't sleepwalk either, but you were, and those are stairs." Galen emphasized his point with a sweeping hand gesture towards the other side of the room. "Falling down them would kill him," he said firmly, as if he were talking to something else.

"Who are you talking to?"

"Whoever the hell it is who is messing with your dreams. I thought they should know!" Galen paced away.

Rob watched him. His brother wasn't usually quick

to anger, so this reaction seemed a little off. He wasn't sure why, but something was worrying. There was a line of tension in Galen's back that spoke of a man going into battle, not someone standing in his home. That's what it was. His brother was already preparing for battle. He knew Galen was worried, the ravens were too. The four of them had talked during dinner, and Dera and Dor had passed along the concerns of the Hunt. *That* was worrying. Considering most things ran in fear from the Hunt, and they had defeated the armies of the *feorhbealu*, the fact they were worried was more than a little scary.

Without realizing it, Rob drifted back into sleep. One minute he was in the living room, watching Galen pace, the next he was back in that landscape, the dark path in front of him.

"Is someone here?" he asked, trying to take control of the dream.

"Come to me."

Rob wasn't sure if he heard the voice or if it was more a compulsion, something tugging at him, pulling him along the path. There were other sounds, now that he paused to listen—sounds of the night, the rustle of some creature through the grass, the cry of an owl, a shrill sound that he was unsure of, some night predator, maybe one that didn't walk his world but only this one.

"Where are you?" He tried again.

"Come to me."

Were they words? He still wasn't sure. The message was clear, he understood it, but he wasn't quite sure how. The path seemed to stretch forever, idly he wondered how long the journey would take. Dream time was different than waking time, and what seemed like hours in one could be an instant in the other. The oily black glow of the path bothered him, it shone with power, but it wasn't the quicksilver light he remembered surrounding Galen, or the supernova of color around Stephen Blake, a member of the fae. This black glow was that of Darkness.

"Come to me."

Rob tried to hurry, tried to follow that call, when suddenly, in a brief instant of shining pain, everything went black.

There was a weight on his chest when Rob woke. He stared up at the slow sweep of the ceiling fan for several minutes, trying to figure out what had happened. The voice had called him, then what? The weight on his chest moved and the next moment, Dor was peering into his eyes, one foot resting gently on his chin.

"How do you feel?" Dor asked softly, concern in his deep bass voice.

"I'm... not sure." He shifted to indicate he wanted to sit up and the raven hopped off him and sat on the table beside the bed, still focused on him. "Why are you here? Shouldn't you be destroying Flash's car or something?"

"I serve My King," Dor chided.

"Oh." Rob felt a blush creep up his cheeks. "Sorry."

"Yes, Galen called, we have watched since his call."

"I'm going to take a shower." Rob stood, still trying to piece together what had happened. He'd been dreaming, then nothing.

"Good."

When Rob went to close the door to the bathroom, Dor hopped in and sat on the sink. "I don't need a babysitter."

"We disagree."

Rob sighed. He wasn't going to win that argument, so he turned on the shower to let the steam heat the small room, then stepped under the spray, hissing when the water hit a sore spot. Looking down, he noticed a bruise on his thigh that hadn't been there the day before. What had happened? He closed his eyes, recalling the dream, and its abrupt end. Galen. It had to be Galen. *Custodes Noctis* could ease people into sleep to prevent shock on the battlefield, and healers' abilities were even more finely tuned. Galen's Gifts were a step above that, among other things he could use the healing like a weapon, and Rob suspected it was something like that which had happened to him. That would explain the faintly nagging headache.

The scent of coffee was filling the apartment when he opened the door, and he could hear Galen singing, his baritone pure and strong. Rob stopped to listen, easily translating the Latin, so when he walked into the room, he wasn't surprised to see candles burning on one of the shelves or several bags with small charms hanging from them on the windowsills, marking the boundary of a protective wall. He slipped past his brother, poured himself a cup of coffee and looked in the refrigerator. There was a container of leftovers from Flash, he pulled them out and set them on the counter for Dor, then leaned back and waited for Galen to finish.

Listening to the words of the spell, he wondered what prompted it. From what he could tell, it was a Bolting spell, creating a protective wall—but the apartment and shop were already protected. Generations of Emrys *Custodes Noctis* had been building on the wall. When Rob had returned home. he'd added a few less common protections and Galen had added his own stamp, which was more than all the others combined. His brother denied it regularly, but Rob knew—had even seen—that his brother had power. Galen had torn down the Veil between the worlds and allowed their motley army through to help the Hunt fight the *feorhbealu* on the fields of the Between World.

When he finished, Galen went and got himself a cup of coffee, silent for a moment. "How do you feel?" he asked, turning to Rob.

"I have a headache."

"You deserve a headache," Galen growled. Dor coughed an agreement and from the top of the bookshelf Dera added a croak of his own.

"What's going on?" Rob sat at the table. Dor hopped over and clung to the back of his chair. "That was a Bolting spell."

"Yes, it was. I have no idea if it's going to help, but I thought we should do something."

"The place is protected."

"Not well enough, apparently," Galen snapped, then took a deep breath. "Sorry." He dropped into the chair across from Rob.

"I was dreaming again?"

"If that's what you want to call it." Galen looked at him. "You were... Sleepwalking all night. Scared the hell out of me."

"Oh."

"We put you back to bed, more than once. I couldn't sleep, so I was in the kitchen when you showed up again. You were bound and determined to get out of here!" Galen got up and paced over to the large plate glass window that overlooked the parking lot and garden. He stood with his back to Rob, leaning his forehead against the window for a long moment before turning back and sitting at the table again. "I decided I had to put you out before something happened." There was something in the way he said it that led Rob to believe it was closer than his brother was letting on.

"I guessed that."

"It was harder keeping you out than it should have been." Galen stared into his cup. "I want to know what we're dealing with, Rob."

"I do too, I have no idea, Galen. I think it called me. I think it said 'come to me', only it was less words and more like a compulsion, like I was being summoned and had no choice."

"We don't like this," Dor said.

"No, we don't," Galen agreed. "I asked Dad for help last night, because I was having such a hard time keeping you down, I thought a boost would help."

"Yeah?" Rob took a drink of coffee. He hadn't sensed his father's presence and usually he did. The elder Keepers had been killed years before, but Galen had called them back into service to face the Old One, and since then, his father and uncle "hung around haunting the place" as his uncle was fond of saying.

"Yeah. There was a little problem, when I called Dad to help, and he tried to get here , he couldn't. Whatever is messing with you is also blocking him from getting to us. The First Emrys couldn't even come through. I tried. I was desperate enough to try the formal ritual of Calling, and they *still* couldn't get here. Whatever we are dealing with can stop that."

"Which is a very bad thing," Dera said softly.

"Very," Dor agreed. *"We are concerned."*

"I'm not concerned, I'm terrified," Galen said firmly. "I've done my best to cast something stronger around our home, but honestly, I don't think it's enough."

"No," Rob said hesitantly. "I guess I don't get to go to Becci's?"

"You don't get to leave the apartment. Not until we know what this thing is. Flash is coming over to play shopkeeper."

"We'll help!" Dera chuckled.

"Help destroy his car?" Rob asked, taking the hint and trying to dispel the tension in the room.

Rob could tell Galen was worried to the point of frantic, and he rarely got that way. One of the things he admired most about his brother was the focus that he brought into any situation. It wasn't really calm, though it might read that way to some people, it was more an intense focus. People often made the mistake that the soft-spoken shopkeeper and guitarist was not a fighter. It was a mistake they only made once. Galen's abilities were remarkable, and since Rob had lost his Gifts and their bond had become muted, they had worked on their fighting technique until they were smoother than many more seasoned Keepers. Rob tried to bring his Gift to bear—sometimes he could get a glimmer from it—and just for a moment he could see the dark wash of worry bordering on fear around Galen. The bond hummed, for an instant that reassuring comfort was there. Rob caught the edges of the exhaustion from his brother—the effort it took to keep even the small spark of the bond alive.

"Come to me." The words were suddenly there, blotting out everything else. Rob could still see Galen sitting across the table, but it was like he was seeing him through a dirty window or curtain. The landscape of his dream was slowly filling up the waking world. *"Come to me."*

"Rob!" Galen said, getting up.

A sharp nip on his neck brought Rob back to the apartment. He blinked and turned to look accusingly at Dor. "Did you bite me?"

"No."

"So that's not blood I feel running down my neck?"

Galen had disappeared, he was back with a towel and bandages. "It's nothing serious,'" he said, swiping it with alcohol. "It shut down the bond, I couldn't reach you at all."

"But I..." Rob began.

"Yeah, as soon as you forced your Gift, it was there, I felt it right before it shut me out."

"What was it?" Rob asked, watching his brother's face. "Galen?"

"It felt like death."

"That's how my dreams were at first. Last night I tried to guide it, and for the first time, I saw more, a landscape, a path. I could see with my Gift there."

"Are you sure it was your Gift?"

"It felt like it." Rob sighed and got up. Galen tensed and both ravens rustled their wings. "Coffee. I am just getting coffee. Then I am going to walk over there," he pointed at the table by the bookshelves, "and I am going to see if I can find out anything more."

"Hey!" The downstairs door banged open. "I'm here!" Flash stomped up the stairs and looked into the room. "I stopped by the stand. Becci said no one had been by this morning. She was worried."

"Rob's grounded," Galen said, smiling.

"Huh." Flash carried a paper cup to Rob and handed it to him. "What'd you do?"

"He tried to fly down the stairs."

"He what? You what?" Flash looked from Galen to

Rob. "Right. So, things are worse than I thought. Okay. Right. Here's your mocha. I'll go open the shop. No flying down stairs," he said to Rob. "And you two leave my car the hell alone."

"Who, us?" Dera said, cocking his head to the side. *"You're helping today, the car is off limits."*

"Yeah, well it fucking well better be." Flash headed downstairs.

"I didn't say anything else was," Dera said, dropping off the shelf and flying down the stairs.

"I'm going to see if I can track this down a little more, Galen, you can go downstairs."

His brother gave him a searching look. A crash sounded from below. "It wasn't anything important!" Flash called.

"Okay, I'll be right back. Dor's going to keep an eye on you."

The raven nodded. Rob waited until Galen was gone before opening the book again. It was early to start in on the ancient text, sometimes it was harder to get his brain to switch on and read the older languages. It usually happened when he was tired. He grabbed the Latin translation of the work and looked at the passage, there was a word he was sure was wrong, so he dragged the modern work over as well, Barry had used the Latin and had the same word, *Satan*, and that wasn't right. Rob turned back to the original and stared at the vellum, carefully going through the entire page.

"Come to me." The page began to blur, the words becoming the oily black shimmering path. He tried to shake it off, but the harder he concentrated, the clearer the path became. Somewhere far away, he thought he heard the concerned call of a raven. The path bid him to

follow, the landscape rolling towards a great cliff, he could see it clearly now. It was huge, dark against the rest of the surrounding hills, the scent of the land filled his senses. *"Come to me."* There was no denying the summons. Rob could only answer.

Pain suddenly cascaded through his body, jarring him, pulling him away from that dark land. Rob tried to struggle up through the pain, he could hear Galen shouting his name, but his brother's voice seemed to be coming from a distance. Something was running over his face, soft droplets of warmth. The harsh call of the ravens was there as well, and he could hear Flash's panicked swearing in the background.

"Rob, what the hell?" Galen said from beside him.

"Galen?" Rob asked, confused. He had no idea where he was, all he knew was pain, everywhere, there were sharp pains and a dull, throbbing ache. There was a small warmth of the healing easing through him, enough to stop what he thought might be the beginning of shock, but he could sense Galen was having trouble.

"I'm going to put you out before I move you."

"Move me? What happened?"

"You went out the window, Rob." Galen's voice was completely calm. Warmth and the sound of a heartbeat filled Rob and he was carried away into a silent, soft darkness.

FIVE

Galen

Galen hadn't seen it coming, had never suspected the attack to come in broad daylight. He felt a tiny *something,* he would never be sure what it was, but something buzzed through the bond, and he was moving towards the back of the shop at a full run before the sound of breaking glass shattered the silence of the Apothecary, cursing himself the whole time for leaving his brother at all.

* * * *

He'd been sure it was safe, he'd made sure Rob was settled with his books, and headed down the stairs. The curtain that led into the front of the shop was partially open and Galen could see Flash bend over, sweeping something into a dustpan. Dera was sitting on a stool just inside the door, watching intently. He gave Galen a little shrug, then turned back to his observation of Flash. Sometimes Galen wondered how his friend managed to break something every time he was in the store, but he did, without fail. Of course he always paid for it, and it was usually nothing important, in fact, Flash had an uncanny ability to break replaceable items, which was a relief.

He was glad he'd called Flash, and not just because he knew the Apothecary was in relatively good hands if he needed to be elsewhere. He'd met Flash when they'd both auditioned for a band, decided they didn't like the other members and set out to form their own. Once they'd found Pete Miles who played drums and his cousin Sean who played keyboard and rhythm guitar, The Urban Werewolves had been born. Over the last few years, they'd been slowly been making their way up the local scene, and playing better venues. The night of the accident, they'd been on the way home from a gig at Hell's Half Acre, one of the most popular spots in town.

But Flash was more than a bass player, lead vocalist and Galen's closest friend. He'd faced the Old One and nearly died. His face and neck still showed the purple scars left by the minions of the creature, and the year before he had calmly faced the armies of the *feorhbealu*. Knowing Flash was there relieved some of the tension that was tightening the muscles in Galen's back.

Whatever was going after his brother was powerful, more powerful than he'd ever dreamed. When he'd called his father the night before, Parry had been unable to come, so Galen had actually performed the Calling, a formal ritual designed to call former Keepers back to serve, and none of them, not even the most powerful, The First Emrys, could get through. It was enough to make Galen begin to panic. If the bond had been functioning, he wouldn't be as worried, he'd have a better grasp of what was going on, and honestly, the muted bond was hard to live with. The energy it took to keep even the small spark there was exhausting and he needed it as much as his brother did.

"I didn't mean to," Flash said, spotting him as he walked into the shop.

"You never do."

"The bird made me."

"Do you really want to start that?" Dera asked with a laugh.

"Are you going to tell me what's going on?" Flash asked, setting the broom aside and picking up his coffee.

"I don't know. Rob's been dreaming... Or he says it's dreams."

"But?"

"But he tried to walk down the stairs, he..." Galen stopped and swallowed. "He was up several times last night, trying to leave, he tripped over the end table once. Didn't wake up. I called Dad, but they couldn't get through at all."

"Hence the extra things and piles everywhere."

"Hence?" Galen chuckled. "Yes, hence. I spent most of the night Bolting the place. I'm not sure it did any good, though."

"Why not?"

"Just a hunch," Galen said, carefully arranging the pens by the cash register.

"Oh, fuck. We are so screwed."

"What?"

"Your hunches. The last one you had was what, about a month ago? And look how well that went."

"It wasn't that bad."

"It wasn't your favorite motorcycle that was

destroyed," Flash grumbled.

"We replaced it."

"Yeah, good thing too, 'getting chomped by monster' is not covered by my insurance."

"You need better insurance."

"Uh huh," Flash said, raising his eyebrows. "And how do I start that conversation. 'Excuse me, do you have the coverage for otherworldly, paranormal or acts of destruction not of this earth?' If they did, the premiums would probably kill me."

"Considering the number of speeding tickets you have, I seriously doubt the other would even put a dent in the rest of it."

"Oh ha ha." Flash frowned. "Now, you going to tell me?"

"I would tell you, Flash. I wish I had something *to* tell you." Galen huffed in frustration. "I am at a loss. Rob finally admitted it's been haunting him for days."

"Haunting? You mean a plain old ghost?"

"Flash?"

"Yeah, right, I know. Sorry. Shutting up. Go on."

"He said it felt like the Old One at firs—" Galen started only to be cut off.

"The Old One?!?" Flash almost shouted. "The Old One? As in the thing that..." He rubbed his neck, where the scars still marred his skin.

"Yes, that one, but he said not quite. He's researching something right now about a war between the Old Powers. He was muttering about it last night in his sleep. I'm not exactly sure what he was talking about—more than half of it was in a language I didn't understand. When he came out of the dream enough to be steered back to bed, he would talk about the Ancient Ones. It's not much help."

"Galen," his friend said gently. "Rob's been on edge since the wreck. I know the loss of his Gift has hurt him more than he lets on, could this be...?"

"What? A psychotic episode of some kind?" Galen growled. "I sincerely doubt Rob having a breakdown could stop Dad or the First Emrys from getting here, or that it would send Billy Hernandez into a panic."

"Rob's shaman friend?"

"Yeah. Whatever this is, Flash, it's serious. And Rob has never been one for sleepwalking. He doesn't sleep much, but when he does, he sleeps."

"Right." Flash nodded. "So, I'm here, you can leave the shop in my capable hands, and go figure this out." He grinned.

"You make it sound so easy."

"And like there is nothing breakable left in the shop," Dera added.

"Shut up," Flash told the raven. Dera cocked his head, obviously considering what to do.

Galen was just opening his mouth to reply when he felt something slither along the muted bond. He had his connection with Rob as open as possible, so he knew the instant whatever it was made contact. Without really thinking about it, Galen was running towards the back. He had just reached the stairs when the massive plate glass window that overlooked the parking lot shattered, and as he wrenched the back door open, he saw Rob hit the concrete. The sickening *thud* was followed by the tinkling of glass like the chiming of tiny bells.

He was beside his brother almost the same instant Rob hit the pavement. Flash was right behind him, swearing profusely. Dor was out the window and Dera landed beside Galen, both of them crying soft encouragement. "Rob, what the hell?" Galen asked, trying to keep his voice calm, all too aware of the pain rolling off his brother in a wave strong enough to make him dizzy.

"Galen?" Rob opened his eyes, the blue fogged, not just by pain, but by something else.

Laying a hand on Rob's arm, Galen tried to get an idea of the extent of the injuries his brother had sustained. He swallowed. It was bad enough to be worrying, the drop had done a lot of damage. "I'm going to put you out before I move you," he said softly. Dera leaned against his side, offering support. Galen closed his eyes and was already focusing the healing into his brother as he answered Rob's questions about his fall. The words just flowed around him, it was a struggle to ease his brother into sleep before shock set in, something was fighting back. When Rob went limp, Galen wasn't sure he was completely responsible for it.

"Help me move him," Galen said, opening his eyes, surprised at how harsh his voice sounded.

"Is that smart? Shouldn't we call 911?" Flash asked, even as he gently slid his hands under Rob's legs.

"Let me see what's going on first, we can always call Mike." Galen carefully lifted Rob's shoulders and they carried him inside the couch at the back of the shop.

Once his brother was settled, Galen knelt beside him and laid his hand on Rob's head and chest, calling up the healing light and letting it flow down his arms. It was like running into a solid wall, it took all he had to keep his hands down and stay focused on what he needed to do. Whatever was there was fighting him, unwilling to let the light heal Rob. Taking a deep breath, Galen changed tactics. While still maintaining the healing, he tried to reach out and identify what was there, without letting on to his presence.

"Come to me." The words—or call, maybe they weren't actually words—were there almost immediately. There was something about the voice that sent a shiver of terror through Galen. *"Come to me,"* it repeated.

"I can't." Rob's answer surprised him. *"Something's wrong, I hurt. I was coming, but I had to stop."*

"Come to me."

"I can't, there is something wrong," Rob repeated.

Galen sensed a change and immediately pulled back, hiding as best he could. The owner of the voice was searching through Rob to see what was going on.

"Your body is broken. You need to heal. Then come to me."

The presence was gone, and suddenly the light flowed easily into Rob. Galen guided it through his brother's body, gently repairing what the two-story fall had done. He could see the spots where the dark tendrils of the thing were beginning to get a foothold in his brother, hiding in the scars left by previous encounters with Darkness. When Galen finally pulled his hands away, dark spots were dancing at the edge of his vision. He walked to the table and sat down, putting his head in his hands.

Dera gently nipped at his hand. *"How bad is it?"*

"Not good, worse than I thought, although I've fixed the physical problems. At least as well as I could. He's going to need time to heal correctly. I am half-tempted to call Mike and get something." Mike Silva was a close friend and emergency room doctor that had come to their aid on more than one occasion.

"I think you should just call him," Flash said, pulling out his phone. "Drug him so he can't go flying out windows."

"If I thought it would make a difference, I would." Galen sighed. The strength of the summons could probably override anything they tried.

"You don't even think it's worth a shot?"

"We must do something," Dor said, his deep voice worried.

"Galen?" Rob asked softly.

He looked up and smiled. "Hey, Brat."

"What happened?" Rob tried to sit up, but collapsed back onto the couch with a groan. "And why am I in the back of the shop?"

"Because we carried you," Flash said, walking over to glare at him.

"What?" Rob looked from Galen to Flash, then noticed the ravens. "What?"

"What do you remember?" Galen stood and walked over, perching on the couch arm.

Rob frowned. "It was calling me again, and it showed me where it was. I was walking towards it when..." He blinked. "Did you say I went out the window?"

"Yeah. Right through the glass," Galen answered calmly, even as his hands started shaking again.

"Right through the glass?" Rob raised his eyebrows. "How much will that cost me?" he asked, the sardonic tone he used to cover emotion in his voice.

"We'll see after I call the glass guy."

"Yeah, I bet." Rob blinked. "I really went out the window?"

"Yes." Galen stood and paced to the still open door, looking out at the broken glass and blood that marked the spot where his brother had fallen. "Right out the damn window."

"But you healed me."

"Rob, the healing... I tried, I couldn't at first. There was something there blocking me. It spoke to you, and you *answered it.*" The last two words snapped out of him with more anger and fear than he planned. His brother, Flash and both ravens stared at him. "You would have died if it hadn't let go."

"Which is not good," Flash added.

"You think?" Galen rounded on him.

"Hey, I'm on your side!"

"Galen, we understand you are upset. This does not solve the problem," Dor said calmly.

"You said I was speaking with it?" Rob interjected.

"Yes, while you were unconscious," Galen replied, his back to them.

"It comes when I sleep too." Rob paused. "And you could hear it?"

"Yeah?" Galen turned back. "Not a good idea."

"What's not?" Flash demanded.

"He wants me to put him out, and see if it talks to him," Galen said.

"You'd be there."

"It might be our best chance," Dor added.

"Do not encourage him!" Galen paced away again. He knew they were fighting a losing battle, and he didn't even know what he was fighting yet.

"This is what we do," Rob said calmly, struggling up. "I need to find out when..." His eyes suddenly unfocused and he took an unsteady step. Galen grabbed his arm and stopped him. Rob tried to pull away, seemingly unaware of his surroundings, but Galen held him in place. Galen carefully opened the bond to get a better idea of what was talking to Rob. The voice was back, the summons so strong, he almost found himself caught up in the call. His brother was answering, the words dissolving quickly into emotion.

Galen tuned out the soft conversation—or whatever it was—between Rob and the thing and tried to get an idea of what was going on. It was important to know who was calling Rob and how much power it actually had. Hiding his presence as best he could, Galen delved deeper, seeking what was there. The answers that shivered up the connection terrified him. It was ancient, and its power had built over the millennia until the very land around it hummed with its existence. Galen gently tried to ease closer to the connection it had with Rob. It was a mistake.

It was aware of him.

Galen felt his brother's panic and desperately tried to pull away, but it was too late. The owner of the voice lashed out at him, reaching him through the connection with Rob. Pain exploded behind his eyes—darkness engulfed him—a darkness smelling of heat, the fires that lurked under the mantle of the earth. In the midst of the smoke and flame surrounding him, the voice was chiding him for trying to find it and stop it. Pain became agony, searing along his skin. The last thing he heard was Rob's voice, in his head and in his ears, begging for his life.

"Galen?" Rob's voice was harsh. "Galen?"

"Rob?" Galen tried to speak but his vocal chords wouldn't respond. He felt a shaking hand on his head.

"Can you heal?" The trembling hand on his forehead didn't move.

"Let me try," Galen said, focusing the healing and sending it through his body. Whatever had happened was serious. He floated there for a moment, drawing on the light. The creature, whatever it had been, had stripped him bare. "I'm... I'm mostly okay," he said, opening his eyes. He was on the floor, Rob and Flash were kneeling beside him.

"It knew you were there," Rob said, sitting back on his heels.

"Yes." Galen pushed himself up and leaned against the couch. He laid a hand on his brother's arm to get a sense of what was going on with Rob. The echo of the thing was still there, a black shadow, hard as stone. The soft buzz of the muted bond was completely gone. Galen felt his heart accelerate in terror, then clamped it down as he eased the connection open.

"I tried to block it from you," Rob said before he could ask.

"Block what?"

"It sensed you and wasn't happy."

"I think not happy doesn't fucking cover it," Flash said. "It tried to kill him."

"Yes, this is not good," Dera said, hopping over to sit protectively on Galen's leg. *"This is far worse than we have considered. It is an Ancient, and one of the Punished."*

"The punished, that just sounds so much better," Flash said.

"They fought a great war, and some were imprisoned. I was working on that when..." Rob trailed off.

"You flew out the window," Flash finished for him.

"Yeah." Rob stood. "I need to finish, find out more, and you need to heal, Galen," his brother said firmly.

"You do too, Brat." Galen let Flash help him to his feet. The Ancient had drained him far more than he had let on, it took everything he had to walk to the stairs without falling. The scar in his chest where the Old One had torn free was throbbing with a new pain, and he was aware of a weakening of his Gift. Rob followed him, and the ravens swept into the apartment ahead of them, Dera landing on the back of the sofa and Dor at the table.

Galen made it to the oversize chair he preferred and dropped down, exhaustion suddenly dragging him into darkness. As he drifted away, he thought he heard his brother speaking with the ravens, the sound of a door closing and sometime later, the distinctive sound of Rob's Jeep's engine starting. Galen jerked awake and stumbled to the window in time to see his brother pull out of the parking lot.

Six

Galen

It took a full second for Galen's brain to catch up with the significance of the car pulling out of the lot. The next moment, he was racing down the stairs. Reaching the back door, he tried to open it, only to find it jammed closed. Without wasting any effort on trying to force it, he turned and ran towards the shop, only to be stopped by a pained groan from a prone body. "Flash!" Galen flipped on the light and dropped beside his friend. There was a dark bruise marring the side of Flash's face.

"Fucker hit me," Flash muttered.

"Rob?" Galen asked as he set his hand on Flash's head to use the healing.

"Yeah." Flash sighed as Galen pulled his hand away. "Thanks, that hurt."

"What happened?" Galen asked.

"Rob came down stairs, I didn't think anything of it, you know? He came into the shop, grabbed something then headed towards the back. I just put a hand on him to see where he was going, and pow."

"Flash?" Galen held up his hand. "Slow down. I need a little more detail."

His friend ran a hand through his hair, pulling loose the band that held the ponytail in place and putting it back in. "Rob came down about fifteen minutes after you went up. Huh."

"Huh?"

"He didn't get coffee, I should have known something was up then. I'm an idiot." Flash shook his head and continued, "He headed over to the books, he was over there for a few minutes, going through them. I really didn't think anything about it, you know? He does that. I should have thought about the no coffee thing, though. Why didn't I see that?"

"Which books?" Galen headed into the shop and over to the research section. Flash trailed after him, muttering the whole time about coffee. "Which ones?"

"That big brown one, the blue one with gold lettering and..."

"And?"

"And that one that isn't right here," Flash said, sliding his hand in an empty space.

Galen looked at the books. Both were collections of Sagas, and the missing one was in the section on geology. He stared at it for a long time, trying to remember what had been there. "I'm an idiot," he said suddenly.

"Glad I'm not alone. Why are you an idiot?" Flash asked.

"They're cataloged."

"What?"

"Rob catalogs all the books."

"Wouldn't we need to know what the book was? Author or something?" Flash asked dubiously.

"You'd think, but this is Rob. He has too much time on his hands most of the time, and tends to over-organize. For once I'm happy about it."

"Why?"

"This." Galen walked over to the old library card-catalog file cabinet his brother had purchased at an auction. "He has them all cataloged here, but by section. So we find the book right before it, which is?"

"Lyell, *The Ancient Changes of the Earth.*"

"Is *Volcanism and Tectonism* by Stephen P. Reidel and Peter R. Hooper there?"

"Nope, the next book is on Krakatoa."

"There's no *Fire, Floods and Faults*?"

"No."

"He took two books, then," Galen slammed the drawer closed. "Why?" He tried to reach out along the bond, only to come up against that solid wall of shadow. He eased back before it became aware of him and lashed out. Judging by the first attack, he would be in serious danger if that happened, and they had to get to Rob.

"Shouldn't we, I don't know, be going after him?"

"Yes! Of course we should!" Galen snapped. "Sorry, we should, but we need to know where we're going and what we are facing."

Flash nodded, pulled out his phone and punched a number. "Hey, yeah. Rob's gone. Yeah. No. Uh huh. Yep. Please. Yeah, and make mine an extra large." He looked up at Galen. "Rhiannon's on the way. I figured we'd need back up."

"Thanks for asking."

"Anytime." Flash grinned. "So what?"

"We see what he was looking for." Galen strode across the floor, heading towards the stairs to the apartment. As he reached the top, he heard an odd noise. "Dera!" he called. An angry croak came from down the hall. Sprinting through the living room, he discovered the door to the bathroom jammed closed, a chair wedged against the knob and the skeleton key that was always in the lock lying on the floor in the hallway. He quickly opened the door and both ravens swept out, croaking angrily, seemingly twice their usual size.

"Where is he?" Dor demanded.

"I don't know. He drove out of the parking lot."

"I go." The raven dipped his head and was out the broken window before Galen could say another word.

Dera landed on his shoulder and gently butted his cheek. *"Are you injured?"*

"No." He walked to the table where Rob had been sitting. There were still books open on the table, paper marking various spots. Galen bent closer to one page, then glanced at another. "Do you think he was trying to leave us clues?"

"How?"

"I don't know. When I healed him, it was there, so maybe he was trying to leave us breadcrumbs?"

"I like that idea, and it is something he might do. Can you read this?" Dera drifted gracefully onto one of the books.

"Not really, although Rob did say that this one," Galen tapped the book in front of him, "was a translation of the one you're on. Not a good translation."

"Of course not," Dera chuckled fondly.

Galen read the passage that was marked and dragged another book over, the whole time the need to go after his brother getting more and more desperate. He could just sense Rob through the bond, the tiniest whisper, fainter than usual, and what was there was beginning to make Galen frantic with worry. "What does this mean?" he asked, reading a paragraph for the fourth time.

"You think I'd know?" Flash asked sourly.

"How long have you been there?"

"Long enough to listen to you muttering about all kinds of shit, none of which made sense."

"I need help, I don't even know where to go. I think he was researching this here: 'and they raged over the whole of the land, churning it beneath their feet, destroying as they moved. Several of their number rose up, and they were punished, they suffered the death that was not death, and they were placed within the living rock.' I'm just not sure where that leads us."

"Are things that are locked in rock things we really want to be looking for?"

"Since I think one of them is what has Rob, yes," Galen said, his eyes straying over the page again.

"I don't like it."

"I don't either."

"Thanks for the..." Galen stopped when his phone rang, he glanced at the caller ID and felt his heart speed up. "Rob!"

"Galen?" Rob sounded confused.

"Where are you?"

"Heading up Snoqualmie Pass."

"Where?"

"I'm not at the summit, but I will be in a few. I don't have long. I... I'll... no, too soon... East, Galen, I'm hea..." The phone cut off abruptly.

Galen stood. "We need to get going. Rhiannon's here?"

"Yeah, Greg too."

"I don't think they need to come." He walked back to his room and opened the closet where he kept his weapons. He pulled out his bag—full of supplies, medical and magical—and his falcata. He didn't know if he'd need it, but he preferred the bladed weapon to a gun, but that didn't stop him from grabbing his Sig Sauer P226 9mm, and tucking it in his bag as well.

When he walked back into the living room, he stopped in front of the shelf on the west wall. The Emrys family Coat of Arms hung there, with a roster of names of Keepers back to the First Emrys thousands of years before. Most importantly, the Swords were there. *Custodes Noctis* blades were special, bonded to the user, and passed from generation to generation. These swords had begun life in the Copper Age and had been carefully improved over the millennia. The blades were etched with a variety of spells, runes, ogham, Latin, each adding strength to the Swords. Galen's panic ramped up a notch when he realized that Rob's sword was still there.

His brother would never go into battle without it.

Galen grabbed both swords and headed downstairs, walking out into the lot towards the 1939 Ford Coupe a long-time customer had given him. He loved the car, and they drove it often. The closer he got to it, to the reality of driving, the more he started sweating. He hadn't driven since the accident; every time he got behind the wheel he would come so close to a panic attack he would have to call up the healing to stop the reaction. It hadn't really been a problem so far, more an inconvenience, but now, faced with not just a drive across town, but possibly across the state... He stopped and attempted to get the panic under control.

"Despite the damage that certain birds have done to

my car, it's far faster than yours," Flash said, coming up behind him.

"Flash..." Galen turned to his friend. "I don't know what I'm heading into."

"And your point would be?" Flash grabbed his arm and tugged him towards the black SUV parked by the wall. "Get in. You too," he said to Dera. "No eating of the upholstery."

"Why would I do that? It doesn't taste good, and it's not fun."

"Ha ha. Rhiannon, we're going!"

A small woman came out the back door. Galen had met Rhiannon Ross when he was eighteen. Her daughter had been killed and since then she had become a killer of things that took children. It was her specialty, although she was willing to join any fight that came her way. She'd stood beside him many times, in many battles. She walked over and hugged him, then pushed him gently into the car. "You both better come back."

"Hey," Flash whined.

"You three. You know exactly what I meant, Flash. You better bring them both home, or I'll have your head for a coffee mug."

"Yes, ma'am."

"I'll have the window fixed, too," she added as she closed the car door. "Be careful, Galen."

"I will," Galen assured her softly.

Flash pulled out and onto the street. "Where to?"

"Head towards the pass, that's where he called from."

"Wouldn't it be cool if you could just track him by his phone like they did on that show last night?"

"It would be, but I think you have to turn on that function..." Galen stopped. "I wonder if he would?"

"You mean if he calls in again? Do you think he'd have time? Before it shuts him down again?" Flash flipped off the driver in the car beside them, passed and merged onto the freeway. "Asshole."

"I'm not sure. It's becoming more and more aware." Galen could sense the solidity of the shadow through the muted bond, it was slowly growing so what he felt of his brother was not Rob, but that dark, ancient power.

"What the hell is your problem?" Flash shouted, swinging into the left-hand lane, racing around the luxury car beside them, then cutting them off to cross all four lanes to get to the Auburn exit. "You know how fast that car can go? And they're poking along at fifty on the freeway. Fifty!" Flash swung around the exit with enough speed to toss Galen against the door and Dera to dig his claws into the seat back.

"Flash!"

"What?" his friend answered innocently. "You want to get there or not?"

"I would like to get there, period."

"Right. That's what I mean." Flash cut off a semi, and slipped into the left-hand lane. Galen watched as the speedometer started to climb, then decided it was probably best to ignore it. "There's a map in the glovebox."

"Map?"

"Yeah." Flash glanced over at him. "I don't trust the GPS in this thing, not since it got me lost that one time."

"You weren't on the road."

"It should have found a road for me," Flash insisted. "Paper also doesn't need a battery. More to the point in this case, if he is headed over east, that thing shows a lot of roads he might use, so maybe if he tells us, we can get an idea of where we need to be."

"Good idea."

"I know." Flash grinned.

Galen opened the map and looked at the lines snaking across it, the colors looking like veins and arteries. Smaller roads were tiny pencil gray lines leading off the brightly colored main roads. He ran his finger along the I-90, trying to see if he could sense his brother through the paper. Scrying had never been something he'd been able to do, but this was different. It was more remote sensing. There was no bounce, nothing to indicate where his brother was, so he let that go and instead just let his eyes roam over the map. For some reason they were drawn, again and again, to a spot on the east side of the Columbia River. There was a tiny gray road that ended abruptly against a mountain. He could see the change in altitude on the map. He glanced up to see where they were, then down at the map and his eyes focused on that spot again.

Hunch? Wishful thinking? He closed his eyes, concentrating, reaching out for his brother. He brushed against the dark shadow and tried to skirt it. Had their bond been what it once was, this wouldn't be a problem—maybe—but now finding his way without any help from Rob was almost impossible. Still, he was getting close, he caught the first whisper of his brother—then sensed the trap.

"You will not stop this." The words screamed in his head and suddenly his blood felt like it was boiling, his flesh was searing off and a knife, serrated and horrible was tearing through his mind. He desperately scrambled away, aware of someone screaming, but all he could think about was getting away. There was an explosion of pain

in his shoulder, he reached out with the healing and shut everything down, protecting himself from the attack.

"I did stop!" Flash snapped as Galen slowly became aware again. A cool cloth brushed against his face and the ground was hard under his back.

"Not fast enough," Dera chided.

"Were you expecting him to jump out the fucking door?"

"No, not really."

"Yeah, well, so there."

"Flash?" Galen asked, opening his eyes. He was on the side of the road, looking up at a huge tree.

"Welcome back." Flash leaned back. "Don't you know jumping out of moving vehicles is not a very good idea?"

"I did what?" Galen cautiously sat up, making sure nothing was broken. In those last seconds when he'd thrown up the healing as a shield, he must have blocked his body from harm—that, or healed it while he was unconscious, either way all he felt was bruised and a little tired.

"You screamed and jumped out of the car. Lucky for you, Dera figured out something was up and told me to slow down so I wasn't going ninety when you opened the door."

"You shouldn't go ninety anyway," Galen said as he stood up, pausing to let a wave of unexpected dizziness pass. He smiled at the raven. "Thank you."

"It attacked you, why?"

"Yeah, that's a good question, why?" Flash asked, opening the door and waiting for Galen to get in. He made a show of activating the child proof lock before closing the door. Dera flew in the driver's door, perched on the seat and fixed Galen with a steely look. "Well?" Flash growled.

"I was trying to reach Rob," Galen said. Somehow that didn't feel right. That wasn't the reason.

"And it didn't want you messing with him?" Flash pulled back on the road, floored it and crossed back into the fast lane, dodging slow-moving semis the whole way.

"I'm not sure." He was about to say more when his phone rang. "Rob?"

"Are you okay? I couldn't stop it."

"Yes. Where are you?"

"Heading east on I-90. I don't know... I..."

"Rob..." Galen stopped, realizing with sudden clarity why he'd been attacked. How could he let his brother know? "I've got coffee."

"You... It better be... Quad... Gal..." And the connection broke.

"You've got coffee? Where?" Flash said, glancing over at him. "I want coffee."

"You know why you were attacked?"

"Yes," Galen said excitedly. "I do."

"Want to tell the rest of the class?" Flash muttered as he ran the car onto the shoulder to pass a slow-moving convoy.

"Thanks to your map, I know where Rob's going."

"What?"

"Yeah, here." Galen pointed to the spot where the tiny gray road ended and felt a small burst of red-hot pain in his head. Whether or not the Ancient One had meant to, it had just confirmed the location. "That's where we're going."

"You're just lucky this thing has four-wheel drive," Flash grumbled.

"How long will it take?"

Flash grinned. "If you keep your eyes closed, not long at all." He laughed and floored it.

SEVEN

Galen

They had been on the road for nearly two hours, the forested Cascades giving way to the open plains of Eastern Washington. In the distance Galen could finally see the haze marking the Columbia River Gorge. The fields were flecked with the first ridges of lava. As they got closer to Vantage, he could feel a soft tug, something pulling him away from the freeway and pointing them towards the huge basalt cliffs along the gorge. The Columbia River snaked through the valley, a deep blue, reflecting the color of the sky. The wind whipped the SUV as they crossed the bridge at Vantage.

Galen had been studiously ignoring the speedometer since Cle Elum, when he'd made the mistake of looking over and seeing it hovering around ninety-five. Once they were past Ellensburg, he knew Flash had sped up even more, and by the time they reached the long downgrade to the river, he guessed they were easily going faster than a hundred. They turned right when they reached the east side of the bridge and started heading downriver. The massive hills rose around them like castles, the lava buttresses hanging out over the road.

Small roads led off into the hills, some of them were marked, most weren't. Galen checked the map again. "Slow down."

"What?"

"Our turn is coming up, if I'm right. We need to go about seven tenths of a mile past the next marker."

"Okay." Flash slowed the car to thirty, his eyes moving between the road and the odometer. "This is seven."

"There's the road," Galen said, pointing to a tiny track to their left.

Flash turned onto the road. About a quarter of a mile up, there was a cattle grate and a gate marking the boundary of public lands. Galen got out and opened the gate. He could smell dust on the air, a car had passed through not long before, the scent was still sharp in the hot sun. Getting back in, he smiled. "I think we aren't as far behind as I thought we were."

"I got us here fast," Flash boasted.

"And Rob was probably trying to fight as much as he could."

"Dor!" Dera cried. *"Open the door!"*

Galen did as he was told, and before he even spotted the other raven, the bird was swooping into the car. "Are you okay?"

"I am. We have to hurry! How did you find us?" Dor asked, looking at the three of them.

"He used my map," Flash said smugly.

"How far is it?"

"I don't know, I flew," Dor said.

"Not very helpful, you know," Flash muttered and

started up the road at a speed that had the tires sliding on the rocks. "Fucking washboard road. That's what happens when idiots who shouldn't be driving out here try driving out here." He had his hands on the wheel and Galen could see his knuckles were white.

"Idiots like you?" Galen joked. He knew Flash was afraid. That was one of the things he admired most about his friend. He was terrified half the time he walked into a fight like this—probably most of the time, and still he was there, backing them up. When he had insisted on riding with the Hunt, he had no idea if he'd survive, and still he stood with them. Galen nudged him gently. "Or other idiots?"

"Other idiots, of course."

They were making turns onto increasingly narrow roads, finally giving way to something that resembled a game track more than a road. Galen heard Flash swear as something dragged along the bottom of the car with a tremendous screech. They were traveling between two huge walls of lava, the way getting harder and harder to navigate. Flash was fighting the steering, trying to keep the SUV up on the narrow track, while the walls got closer and closer.

"If I wasn't sure Rob had gone through here in that Jeep of his, I would stop," Flash said as a rock scraped along the driver's side door.

"He did, with his eyes closed," Dor said.

"Oh, that makes me feel better. Shut up." Flash nearly lost control when one wheel dropped into a deep hole as the road made a hairpin turn. He wrenched the car back up onto the track. Galen breathed a sigh of relief. He had never fully realized how good a driver Flash was until that moment. The walls got closer and closer until

Galen was holding his breath, listening to the scrape of metal against rock as Flash negotiated the road. When he was sure they couldn't go any further, it suddenly opened up into what at first appeared to be a box canyon, with dark basalt walls all around. It was only when Galen took a second look at the south-facing wall that he noticed a crevasse and the dark sheen of glass.

"Galen," Flash said softly. "There's the Jeep." He pulled up beside it.

It took all of the discipline Galen had to keep from jumping from the car and searching for his brother. No *Custodes Noctis* would walk into a situation like this one blind and unarmed. They needed a plan, and probably a contingency plan. Dera nudged him.

"Flash, Dor, Dera, I need you to wait here until I call," Galen said firmly.

"No."

"No."

"No."

"I need you to stay behind me to back me up, until I need help."

Flash looked back at the ravens. The three of them looked at Galen, then nodded. "Okay, but if anything looks even a little wonky, we're coming in," Flash said.

"Wonky?" Dor said. *"Always eloquent."*

"It's a technical term, I wouldn't expect you to know," Flash said haughtily.

"We need to go, where is Rob, Dor? Do you know?"

"He went towards the wall of glass."

Galen stepped out of the car. The power bubbling beneath his feet boiled up his legs and knocked him to the ground. He felt the sharp bite of stones as his knees hit the earth. Flash was out of the car and dragging him to his feet before he had a chance to even process what was going on. Once he was standing, he tried to ignore the dark pulse beneath him. It filled the whole area, beating in time with his heart, twisting at the scar the Old One had left in his body. His first step was more a stumble, but he leaned on the side of Flash's car and walked around to the back.

Flash opened it and Galen grabbed the Emrys Sword that was his and buckled it on, the baldric holding it tight against his back, its soft song a counterpoint to the dark beat in the stones. He buckled Rob's on as well, his brother wore his Sword in a belt, preferring to carry his every day blade—a massive bastard sword—in a scabbard on his back. Galen had a feeling they might need the power of the blades for what was coming. Flash grabbed the medical bag and his own weapon of choice, a massive war hammer. He'd chosen it when he'd discovered he lacked the patience to become proficient with a sword. However, as he was fond of saying, finesse was not needed for "whacking things."

Galen smiled at Flash and set out across the broken rock, aware that each step was harder to make. As he reached the opening, he got his first look at Rob. His heart nearly stopped. His brother was standing against a massive wall of obsidian, shining dark in the sun. His face was bloody, there were cuts on his forehead and hands, his t-shirt had dark red stains as well. Rob's arms were outspread and he was pressed against the surface, almost like he was hugging it. Galen slipped silently up beside his brother. Rob's eyes were closed, his face a mask of agony.

As he drew closer, Galen realized the stone, while it looked like volcanic glass, was something else. It glittered in the sun, sparkling like the rainbow on an oil slick, and the warmth he felt was coming from the rock, not the sun. All around him the wind was sighing, and then it hit him. It wasn't the wind. It was the sound of the mountain. It was breathing.

The power here was immense. It thrummed through Galen, a deep bass note rattling through his bones. Rob was speaking softly, words Galen didn't understand, and the mountain was distracted. Without drawing attention to himself, Galen started to carefully siphon off some of the energy that was under his feet, that was filling the scar in his chest and beating in his head with a searing intensity. With each slow breath he took, he drew a little more, not much at any time, and as he did so, he crept as close as he could to Rob without his brother becoming aware of him. When he thought he had enough strength to do it, Galen reached out and with a hard, violent grasp, yanked his brother from the wall.

The soft sighing whisper of the wind—the breath of the mountain—changed to a roar of rage. "What have you done?" The rocks grated together, creating the sound. Galen looked up in shock. Before he'd only heard the voice in his head, but now the sounds hammered against his ears in with painful beat. Stones broke loose and rained down on them.

"Rob?" Galen looked into his brother's eyes. There was nothing there, the slate-blue focus was gone. Galen drew on the mountain again, using his own healing and the creature's energy to force his brother free psychically as well as physically. He saw a spark of recognition in Rob's face. "Rob?"

"Galen?" Rob asked, confused. He looked around. "Where?"

"You with me?" Galen insisted, dragging his brother's gaze back to his own.

"Yeah, I think, I..." The focus began to flicker out again, Rob pulled away, took a stumbling step and before Galen could stop him, was drawn to the wall again with enough force to tear through the fabric of Rob's shirt and leave a deep gash.

"No!" Galen shouted. He drew on the power that was rumbling around him, the rock of the mountain was shifting with anger. Stepping back to Rob, he used a needle-sharp shaft of the healing to wedge himself between the living stone and his brother. As soon as he felt the light touch his brother's mind he pulled Rob away, shoving him as far as he could from the massive glass wall that towered hundreds of feet over their head. Galen kept the sharp focus of the healing, blocking the thing from his brother. Great stones were slamming together just under the surface, the floor of the canyon had begun to shake with the fury vibrating around them. With a final breath, Galen broke his brother free. Rob blinked and his eyes focused on him again.

"How did you do that!" the wall screamed. Galen ignored it.

"Rob?"

"Galen!"

"How did you do that!" the wall shouted again.

Galen tugged at his brother's arm. "We have to get out of here."

"I need to stay," Rob said in a dreamy voice. "I'm of no use anymore, here I can be."

"What?" Galen shook him, hard.

"I can help here, without my Gifts I am a liability."

"Rob!" Galen growled. "Listen to me. We are *Custodes Noctis,* Keepers, and two, always two."

"Yes, your life will be lost," the stones around them said.

"No! You said he wouldn't die!" Rob walked to the wall and stared at it.

"If you die, Rob, I die. It's the way it works."

"The bond is mostly gone, Galen, and he said that I would be here, alive..."

Galen grabbed his brother's arm and yanked him around to face him. "No, Rob, that's not alive."

"It is why I summoned him. I need his heart, his soul, to sustain me. I have waited long, long millennia for him. The one who lives yet does not."

"He is alive," Galen growled.

The mountain laughed at him.

"Rob comes with me."

"You cannot leave," the stones grated.

"Galen," Rob began, edging closer to the wall again.

"No!" Galen snapped then took a deep breath, and shoved his brother away again.

"How did you do that?"

"Do what?" Galen finally demanded, growling at the wall.

"Stop him. You should not be able to stop him."

"I'll stop him again, too," Galen vowed.

It was suddenly quiet. The wind sighed as if the mountain was taking slow breaths thinking about something. A small tremor ran beneath their feet.

"Get out while the getting is good!" Flash shouted.

"No, we must wait," Dera said.

"Galen Emrys," the mountain said. "I have a question for you."

"Yes?" Galen asked suspiciously.

"You know what I am?"

"An Ancient One."

"The *Ealdféond*," Rob said.

"That is what they call me, I have another name," the wall said with wry humor. "They encased me here because I chose a different path." Something buzzed though Galen like the touch of lightning. He dropped to one knee, gasping for breath, a pulse of pain slamming in the scar left by the Old One. "You have met something like their kind."

"I have." Galen struggled to his feet. "And I destroyed it."

"Tell him about the other things," Flash said, sounding like he was much closer.

"Other things?" The voice was curious now.

"He means the *feorhbealu*, we fought them with the Hunt," Rob said quietly. "One of them took my Gifts."

"Ah, yes, I think I know which one it would be, where is it?"

"The *feorhbealu*?" Galen laughed. "We killed it."

"I will ask you then, Galen Emrys, you do not wish your brother here with me?"

"Well, that's a dumb ass question," Flash muttered.

"Not helping," Galen said over his shoulder, then gazed up at the wall of glittering stone. "Of course not."

"Would you free me?"

"What?" The question came from four throats, Galen, Flash and the ravens.

"I believe that you can free me, Galen Emrys, I believe that the time has come, finally it has come, not for me to continue here, but to walk in the light again."

"That so doesn't sound like a good idea," Flash said.

Galen walked past Rob, making sure he kept himself between the mountain and his brother and laid his hand on the wall. Closing his eyes, he opened himself a tiny bit to what was there. He understood that the Old things that walked the earth had different morals, and were not bound by the ethics of humanity, but he had to know that what he let loose would not destroy the world. Galen had long suspected the world was changing, and every encounter they had pointed to those changes. The things that the world had forgotten—that the *Custodes Noctis* had forgotten—were rising. They would need allies. Or, if not allies, those that had once stood against the other forces, the darkness that was coming. Galen sensed this was one such creature. Perhaps not *good* by the definitions of the world, but a potential enemy of his enemies. Satisfied, he stepped back.

"I will free you, Ancient One, as long as I have your word that my brother is free."

The stones laughed. "My word? It is given, for all that it means."

"Fuck no, Galen!" Flash shouted, the ravens were calling too, but Galen didn't know if it was encouragement or anger. All he knew was Rob was fading before his eyes, he could see it, sense it when he made contact.

"Are you sure, Galen?" Rob asked him.

"If you have a better idea? Saga?"

"No."

"Then this is what we do." Galen took off the belt and handed his brother his Sword, then drew his own. The stones around them began to hum in anticipation.

Words began flowing into his head. The power in the earth responded to them as they formed, before they even became sound, the thought itself became a pattern. He stepped closer to Rob and began siphoning the power again, this time openly, drawing it into himself. Galen lifted his sword and cut his arm. "This blood flows, and seeks the earth." He nodded to Rob and his brother repeated his movements and the small incantation. The world shifted, he thought he felt Rob's hand on his shoulder. The words continued in his head, then broke loose, building around them in a song. Images and sensations began to pierce him, the land around them bubbling with fire, agony as the liquid stone flowed over his body, the slow creeping cold of ancient ice, crushing down, stealing his breath until every second was an eternity, and eternity a second. All of it wafted through him like the sighing breeze in the canyon.

It was too late to stop when Rob reached out and placed Galen's left hand over Rob's heart.

"No," Galen said, trying to pull away.

"Only way, Galen," Rob answered with a small, knowing smile.

The power hummed through the stone, filling them both until they were nothing but a small note in the overall song.

The song began to change and Galen began to sing, words so ancient their meanings had long since been lost drifted from his lips. He could feel pain radiating out of Rob, flowing into him as their bond snapped into place, as it had always been. For a brief moment, Rob was there, completely present with him. The bright white light of Rob's heart glowed, the dark scars Galen had healed years before, shadows in the bright sun. The power built, Galen continued to draw it up, he could feel it spiraling around them, rising above them like a tornado to the height of the massive wall. Galen held on, until finally when the vortex was whipping around them, blocking all else from them, Galen let it go, grabbing the swirling power and, using the power of the earth and the bright light of the healing and Rob's heart, forced it outwards into the breathing stone in front of them.

Time stopped.

For an instant everything stopped. The world, the lazy drift of clouds over their head, their hearts. It all stopped for an instant of agony.

"Rob!" Galen said, snapping back to the world. "No!" Rob's heart hadn't started again. "Rob!" The spell had pulled the Gift from Galen, he tried to start Rob's heart but the healing wouldn't respond. "Flash!" he shouted. "CPR!" Flash was there an instant later and they began working on Rob. *Gods dammit, Rob. Come on!* The bond was gone again, only the merest whisper left in the back of his head, but he shouted nonetheless, hoping to reach his brother somehow.

The hum was still filling the canyon, the tone changing, a deep bass grating against a higher note, the single note becoming a chord that made Galen's bones ache. He stayed focused on Rob, counting the compressions, anxiously waiting for the first glimmer of life—or his healing—to return. He thought he caught movement out of the corner of his eye, but dismissed it as just a shower of small rocks.

"Galen!" Flash gasped between breaths. "The fucking mountain is moving."

Galen looked up, the entire wall of stone was undulating, moving as if something was drinking in huge gulps of air.

"Oh shit, Galen, this is..."

"Run," Galen said, dragging his brother up. Flash pulled Rob's other arm over his shoulder and they ran. They made it as far as Rob's Jeep before the hum reached a point of physical pain and there was a huge *crack*, as if the earth were tearing itself open. They stopped and turned, still supporting Rob's lifeless body, in time to see the whole mountain move. Galen was entranced as the stones shifted, shimmering in the sunlight. Small rocks began falling to the ground in a slowly building shower. He was holding his breath when the wall fell completely away. A huge piece bounced down too close for comfort and smashed into Flash's car, spraying them with glass from the windshield. Flash didn't even comment. He was staring up at the mountain as well.

"I am free." The voice was no longer a grate of stone on stone, but a great shout of triumph aimed at the sky. Massive wings, black like a raven's, shining in a thousand colors, opened over their heads as the creature tore itself from its prison. The huge wings swept down, filling the canyon with gale force winds, whipping stones into the air. 'I am free," he repeated, his voice dropping. He turned his great head towards Galen and something like a smile ghosted across its face. With a sound that rattled the cliffs around them, the creature stretched, massive wings spanning the canyon, the claws of his hands and feet glittering in the sunlight and the dark skin, broken by fissures of color, shone brightly for a moment. The *Ealdféond* walked towards them, claws tearing away chunks of ground as he approached.

He stopped in front of Galen and Flash, lifted his huge hand and gently cupped Rob's chin. One claw dropped down and covered Galen's hand where it rested on Rob's chest. Galen felt a jolt of power, his brother tensed and suddenly Rob was gasping in shuddering breaths. He opened his eyes and pulled himself free of their grasp. Galen stepped in front of him, half blocking him from the Ancient One. He could see Flash keeping a hand hovering close to Rob in case he fell.

"You freed me," the Ancient One said.

"I did," Galen snarled.

"Uh, should you talk to, uh, mountains that way?" Flash said *sotto voce.*

A deep chuckle boomed around them. "This is not a gift I take lightly. His heart will sustain me for long millennia."

"Heart? What?" Flash demanded.

"He has part of my heart," Rob said quietly.

"What the fuck? I didn't hear anything about getting part of his heart."

"A spark, a gift, willingly given. I will not soon forget this. I owe you a debt, Robert Emrys."

"The debt is owed to Galen," Rob added.

"Yes." The *Ealdféond* focused on him. "A great debt. I thank you," he said solemnly, brushing Galen with a feather-light touch of a claw. Something sparked in Galen's chest. He felt the warmth of the healing burst back to life, with something else sparkling at the edges of it.

"Can you..." Galen trailed off

"No, I regret, I cannot yet repair what the *feorhbealu* did. There will come a time when you may need me, may need this. I will come."

"I understand," Galen whispered, even though disappointment hammered against his chest.

"We will meet again." A great sigh left the Ancient One's lungs. He gently tapped Rob's chest with the huge shining claw, then lifted his wings, and with a ground-shaking leap, rose into the sky. He hovered above them for a moment, the draft from the wings whistling through the canyon like a song, then disappeared behind a cloud.

Rob started to fall. Flash grabbed him and eased him to the ground.

"Can you help?" Dor asked worriedly.

"Good question," Flash muttered

Galen took a deep breath, the Gift was there, strong and sure. He laid his hand on Rob's head, trying to get an idea of how much damage had been done—and if he had any hope of healing it. He guided the healing through Rob, trying to repair his heart. Once he'd done all he could manage at that time, he took as much of the pain away as he could. "Rob?"

"Hey," Rob said, patting Galen's hand.

"Rob, thank gods." Galen sank down beside his brother and rested his back against the Jeep.

"Scared the hell out of us." Flash leaned on the other side. The ravens perched on Rob's legs.

"How am I?" Rob asked

"You're okay for right now," Galen said softly. Rob's heart was still damaged, it would take time to heal it all the way.

"For right now?' Rob blinked at him.

"I'm killing you later."

"Me too," Flash added.

"We won't," Dor said, glaring at Flash.

Rob chuckled. "As long as you wait a while. I have a headache."

"You deserve a headache after that." Galen took a deep breath. Rob tried to sit up, Galen helped him lean against the car. Rob closed his eyes for a minute. "My chest hurts."

"I probably broke a rib doing CPR." Galen felt drained of everything. "I tried to fix it, but I was focused on..." He stopped.

"How bad is my heart?"

"Bad? What?" Flash looked from Galen to Rob. "He's not fixed? What the fuck?"

"It will heal," Galen sighed. "It's going to take a while."

"The *Ealdféond* left something behind, I'm not sure what, but I can feel there's something different."

"Yeah, I know, I felt it while I was healing you. I don't know what it is—he gave me a similar spark before he left." Galen was quiet, trying to sense just what it was that was there, humming softly in his body.

"I'm sorry," Rob said softly.

"Nothing to be sorry for, Rob."

"You could have died.'

"You did," Galen said, acknowledging what had happened with something that sounded almost like a sob.

"Yeah, I did," he said, meeting Galen's eyes.

"Yeah."

"But I'm better now," Rob said, a slow grin spreading across his face.

Galen frowned for a moment, then felt an answering smile on his own, remembering when he'd spoken those words to his brother. He started laughing.

"What's so funny?" Flash asked.

"Nothing."

"Oh, okay. We should..." Flash broke off. Galen looked at his friend, Flash was staring straight ahead at the smashed remains of his SUV. "My car! What the fuck! My car!"

"We didn't do it!" Dera said quickly.

"You didn't..." Flash stood up and walked over, staring down at a piece of mirror.

"Smashing it wouldn't be fun," Dor said.

"It might be," Dera chuckled.

"We'll get you another one, Flash," Galen said.

"Yeah, you will. And one that's raven proof, and mountain proof and chomping proof and everything else proof. And you..." Flash pointed at Rob. "The next time some damn mountain decides to give you a call, you just hang up."

Galen couldn't help it. He chuckled and heard Rob's answering laugh. Flash stared at them for a moment longer then joined them, dropping back onto the ground beside them, laughing until tears were running down their faces and they were gasping for air. Their laughter slowly eased, drifting off into the sky.

"Ready to head home?" Galen finally said. The sun had set, the night cool around them.

"Yeah, I think so."

Flash stood and opened the back of the Jeep, putting their weapons in the back and shutting it, then holding the back door so the ravens could fly in and settle on the back of the seat. Galen helped his brother onto his feet and they turned for one last look at the place where the *Ealdféond* had rested for so long. Rob glanced at him with a soft smile. Galen smiled back, aware of a small ache in his body. He wasn't sure what it meant, but he saw Rob rubbing his chest as well. Galen sighed, helped his brother into the Jeep and then got in the backseat beside him. Flash glanced at them, then turned on the ignition and headed out of silent canyon towards home.

THE END

THE

BIRTHDAY

A CUSTODES NOCTIS
SHORT STORY

The rich scents of herbs drifted through the warm air in the Apothecary as Galen put back a jar of Elderflower and fussed with it until it was in line with the others on the shelf. Fussing was usually his brother's job, but Rob... He glanced worriedly at the ceiling. Rob was okay, he knew that, could even feel it through the very muted bond they now shared, still he worried. A soft chuckle announced the presence of Dera.

"He is doing well," the raven said softly in his deep voice. Galen had gotten used to hearing him now, and often expected other creatures to answer him. *"And admit it, they do sometimes to, don't they? Not as clearly as I, but they do."*

"Maybe, sometimes," Galen chuckled. The raven

fluffed his feathers at him and hopped along the counter towards him before reaching under the edge and coming up with something shiny. "Stealing from Flash again?"

"Not this time," Dera said. *"I have something for you."* He skipped closer and held up the small amulet.

"What's this?"

"Happy Birthday."

"Thank you, I wasn't expecting..." Galen smiled.

"That I would remember the day? It has been the Emrys birth date for more than four thousand years, since before ever I was born and you think I would forget?"

"Sorry." Galen grinned. "What is it, who'd you steal it from?"

"Me? Steal?" The raven looked offended for a moment then laughed. *"Paracelsus."*

"Paracelsus? *The* Paracelsus?" Galen looked at the metal object a little closer. "Really?"

"He left it by the window. He didn't need it anyway."

"And you just decided that for him?" Galen asked with a smile, the raven bobbed his head. "Of course you did, silly question." He leaned against the counter and listened to the quiet around them. The shop had been busy that morning, but as the day wound on, people headed home to get ready for Halloween parties and trick or treating. Flash knew never to book the band on Halloween so Galen had the night off.

"He is fine, resting last we checked, close the shop, get a coffee and take a short walk." Dera made a little noise that sounded like "murph" in his throat. *"Go, we watch."*

Galen took a deep breath to protest, then changed his mind, he could "hear" the soft hum through the muted bond, his brother was resting, or doing something so his mind was at ease. Lost in research perhaps. It seemed like a lot of his time was lost in books lately, always looking for something that might restore his full Gift. Since their encounter with the *Ealdféond* several months before, Rob had returned to his research with renewed vigor. Not just his usual obsessive need to know, but searching through the Sagas to find a way to return the Gift to what it had been. Rob was convinced they were going to need it, the signs of something shifting in the world were becoming more and more apparent.

Galen believed the things they fought were becoming more common again. The world was shifting. Rob had a theory about that. Galen snorted, of course his brother had a theory about it, not only a theory, but hard scientific evidence, mythology and literature to back it up as well. He laughed. Rob's enthusiasm for research occasionally filled their apartment with an actual palpable warmth, and energy with a life all its own.

Closing the door of the shop behind him, Galen decided to skip the coffee and just wandered down the street, enjoying the smells of autumn. It was his favorite season, something about the way the scents mingled together and the chill on the air, it set a glowing joy singing in his heart that left him smiling happily at the children walking past in costume. On the way out, he'd grabbed a large bag of chocolate and offered pieces to the various witches, Ironmans, werewolves, princesses, several blue Avatars and one green and purple thing he wasn't sure about but it had a crown and the little girl giggled when he offered her a peanut butter cup.

In a much better frame of mind, he stopped in Gateway to India and got a chai tea to go, reveling in the scents of fennel, cardamon and ginger and headed back towards home. He went around back when he arrived, pausing in his garden he sat down on the bench and let the last of the stress slide away. He knew part of it was the effects of the garden. The magic he'd worked into the soil along with the fertilizer and seeds swirled around him wrapping him in a blanket of comfort. The earth was wet and the mints still gave off their strong smell, peppermint and lemon balm warring for the upper hand. The gray mullein towered above the mallow, some of it dying back, some patiently waiting to be harvested.

Movement caught his eyes, Dor landed on the fire escape and hopped through the window, something clasped in his talons. Galen wondered where the bird had been and hoped it had been an errand for Rob rather than a raid on Flash's new car. After losing his to a large piece of the mountain the *Ealdféond* had been trapped in, Galen and Rob had replaced it. For some reason only fathomable to thousand year old ravens, Flash's new car was an even better source of continual amusement. If it made Rob laugh, Galen approved.

He sighed. His brother was recovering, but it had been a close call. Some days it felt like they lived their life from one close call to another. The problem with this one was that Rob was right in his nearly bitter pronouncement that if his Gift had been functioning correctly and their bond at full force it would never have happened. Galen smiled, Rob usually followed up that little bit of bitterness with "right or wrong, it is, and we have to live with it. We'll find an answer." Rob's moments of bitterness were not long-lasting, he continued on, without his Sight, with the muted bond and kept looking for answers.

Galen stood and stepped out of the protective curtain

of the garden, feeling the soft, far-off hum of the bond in the back of his awareness. It was buzzing a little. He quickened his steps and headed into the building and up the stairs. Both ravens were laughing and he could hear his brother joining them as well. When he opened the door, silence fell like someone had hit a switch.

"Galen," Rob said, smiling.

The ravens both barked-chirped.

"Rob?" Galen asked. "You all look...innocent."

"Us?"

"Never!" Dera assured him, offended.

"Yeah, what?" Galen stepped to Rob, his brother looked a little pale. He laid a hand on his head and let the healing flow, feeling the warmth course through Rob's body, driving the pain away and for a moment, the bond was there. Strong, warm, comfortable. He sensed rather than heard Rob's sigh, the ravens hummed. "You've been up too long."

"You are a pain in the ass."

"Everyone is going to be here in about half an hour," Galen said.

"Is Flash bringing his latest brilliant drink invention?"

"Clang? Yeah, I'm afraid so."

"You know I might have to kill him," Rob said with a smile. "It wouldn't be so bad if he didn't have to hit a pan every time he finished a shot."

"But then it wouldn't be Clang."

"Flash logic, he should teach a course, make some philosophy student's head explode."

"I've thought that myself." Galen laughed. "I'll be right back."

"Me too," Rob said and followed Galen towards the

back of the apartment.

When Galen got back to the table there were two packages on the table. He set the two he had down as well. There were other presents in the pile on the couch to be exchanged at the party, but they always took a moment to exchange something special before the party. It was part of their Tradition. The gifts having a meaning the other party-goers might not understand.

Dera was pulling at the ribbon on one of the packages. "Hey! At least let me open them." Galen grumbled

"You said I could get us coffee," Rob added.

The raven looked unapologetic, hopped off the package and waited patiently. "I think they know what's in them."

"I think they do," Rob replied, setting a cup of coffee in front of Galen. "This one first." He handed a long one to Galen.

Carefully pulling off the mylar ribbon and handing it to Dera, he opened the package and looked inside. It was a knife, the blade copper, the handle silver, and the runes of a spell covered the length of the blade.

He looked up at Rob. "Where did you...?"

"I read a description of it in the Saga of the Winter King, the Gathering Knife of the Healer. It was a little difficult to find someone to work the spell into the blade, but it is there, ready for you to make your own."

"This one." Galen couldn't wait and handed Rob a square package. "They actually go together, so open the top one then the bottom one."

"Okay." Rob pulled the ribbon with sparkling stars off and handed it to Dor, then tore the paper off. He pulled the small harp out and looked up at Galen and without waiting ripped open the other package, gently turning the ancient book over in his hands. "The Songs of Taliesin?"

"It's only a Thirteenth Century edition. They are meant to be sung, like all the Sagas, and you always do sing. I thought you should have a harp to accompany you."

Rob was squinting at the harp an odd unfocussed look Galen recognized as his brother trying to use the Gift of Sight. Rob looked a moment longer then up at Galen, his eyes shining. "You made it." The smile that lit his face reminded Galen of his brother as a child, his heart light, and the laughter that rang out through their apartment was every bit as joyful as it had been. "My harp. I..."

"It's Tradition isn't it?" Galen asked. He knew it was, and knew that for his brother the Tradition would make it mean that much more. In times past, as Rob was fond of saying, the elder brother bestowed a harp on the younger brother. Symbol of his role as holder of history, adviser, bard. The harp had magical qualities as well, the longer it was used the more power it gained. At his death the harp would be destroyed and the pieces buried with him.

"You made it?"

"Yes, I chose the wood, and the spell, made the oils and tuned it for your voice." Galen smiled gently. "You keep the Sagas, Rob. You keep Tradition."

"Yes." Rob took a somewhat unsteady breath, tears bright in his eyes. "Well, I should have given you this first, since there is no way I can ever top what you just gave me..." Dera and Dor chuckled. "But here." He pushed a package across the table. "Because of everything that's happened this year, I thought you should have something special."

Galen picked it up, it was obviously a book. He glanced up at his brother, Rob and the ravens looked back with suspicious innocence. Not sure what the looks were about he carefully untied the ribbon and offered it to the ravens. They refused it and waited. Galen unfolded the paper and turned the book over in his hands. Sixteenth Century judging by the look of it, although he could be off by a century.

"You got me a copy of Galen?" Galen cleared his throat. He had several, but none this old.

"Look inside, at the inscription."

Galen carefully opened the cover and stared at the name scrawled in the book. His hands started shaking.

"It's genuine, Galen, I checked and rechecked."

"But Rob..." He looked up at his brother and smiled, ignoring the tears on his cheeks. "It's real?"

"It is. Seemed fitting, you know? You're named for them both."

"I...." Galen swallowed. "Thank you."

"Thank you."

"Happy Birthday, Brat," Galen said, brushing the tears away.

"Happy Birthday, Galen," Rob said, gently running his fingers over the harp strings.

The downstairs door banged open, breaking the mood. Galen reverently touched the signature *"Nicholas Culpepper"* before gently closing the book and putting it carefully on the shelf.

"Get down here! There's Clang to carry!" Flash called.

Rob groaned and Dor and Dera took off with a happy noise. Galen knew they were headed straight for Flash's car.

THE END

About the Author

Born in California, Muffy Morrigan began her writing career at the age of six, when after completing her first hand written novel she attempted to sell it to the neighbors for the lofty price of ten cents. After myriad careers, including archaeological consultant, teacher, herbalist, shop keeper, news editor, reporter and columnist, she has settled in to her first love and passion--writing. She currently lives and works in the Pacific Northwest.

www.muffymorrigan.com

Made in the USA
Charleston, SC
30 March 2012